The Way of the Wicked

The chronicles of Hugh de Singleton, surgeon

The Unquiet Bones
A Corpse at St Andrew's Chapel
A Trail of Ink
Unhallowed Ground
The Tainted Coin
Rest Not in Peace
The Abbot's Agreement
Ashes to Ashes
Lucifer's Harvest
Deeds of Darkness
Prince Edward's Warrant
Without a Trace
The Easter Sepulchre
Master Wycliffe's Summons
Suppression and Suspicion
A Polluted Font

MEL STARR

The seventeenth chronicle of Hugh de Singleton, surgeon

The Way of the Wicked

Published by
Marylebone House
www.spckpublishing.co.uk/marylebone-house
Part of the SPCK Group
Studio 101
The Record Hall
16–16A Baldwin's Gardens
London
EC1N 7RJ

ISBN 978 1 91067 478 9
e-ISBN 978 1 91067 479 6

First edition 2024

Acknowledgments

Scripture quotations taken from the New King James Version®. Copyright © 1982 by Thomas Nelson. Used by permission. All rights reserved.

A catalogue record for this book is available from the British Library

Typeset by Fakenham Prepress Solutions, Fakenham, Norfolk
First printed in Great Britain by Clays, Bungay, Suffolk
eBook by Fakenham Prepress Solutions, Fakenham, Norfolk

For friends and loyal readers at Light and Life Park

"The way of the wicked is like darkness."
Proverbs 4:19

Acknowledgments

In 2007, when he learned that I had written an as-yet unpublished medieval mystery, Dr. Dan Runyon, Professor of English at Spring Arbor University, invited me to speak to his fiction-writing class about the trials of a rookie writer seeking a publisher. He sent sample chapters of Hugh de Singleton's first chronicle, *The Unquiet Bones*, to his friend Tony Collins at Lion Hudson. Thanks, Dan.

Tony has since retired and Lion has joined SPCK, but many thanks to Tony and those at Lion Hudson who saw Hugh de Singleton's potential.

Dr. John Blair of Queen's College, Oxford, has written many papers about Bampton history. These have been valuable in creating an accurate time and place for Hugh.

In the summer of 1990, Susan and I found a delightful B&B in Mavesyn Ridware, a medieval village north of Lichfield. Proprietors Tony and Lis Page became friends, and when they moved to Bampton they invited us to visit them there. Tony and Lis introduced me to Bampton and became a great source of information about the village. Tony died in 2015, only a few months after being diagnosed with cancer. He is greatly missed.

Glossary

Adz: a tool with an arched blade, similar to an ax, used for cutting or shaping large pieces of wood.

Ambler: an easy riding horse, because it moved both right legs together, then both left legs.

Angelus: a devotional celebrated at dawn, noon, and dusk, announced by the ringing of the church bell.

Arbolettys: a cheese and egg custard.

Bailiff: a lord's chief manorial representative. He oversaw all operations, collected rents and fines, and enforced labor service. Not a popular fellow.

Banns: a formal announcement of intent to marry, made in the parish church for three consecutive Sundays.

Beadle: a manor official in charge of fences, hedges, enclosures, and curfew. Also called a hayward.

Beans yfryed: a dish of beans, onions, and garlic. Ingredients were boiled, then fried in oil or lard.

Book of hours: a devotional book, usually elaborately illustrated.

Braes: medieval underpants.

Candlemas: February 2. This day marked the purification of Mary. Women traditionally paraded to church carrying lighted candles. Tillage of fields resumed this day.

Chauces: tight-fitting trousers, often of different colors for each leg.

Coney in cevy: rabbit stewed with onions, breadcrumbs, and spices in wine vinegar.

Coppice: to cut back a tree to stimulate growth of young shoots from the roots. These were used for anything from arrows to rafters, depending on how much they were permitted to grow.

Corn: a kernel of any grain. Maize, American corn, was unknown in Europe at the time.

Corrodian: an individual who received recompense such as food, fuel, even accommodation, in the monastery in return for past gifts to the community.

Cotehardie: the primary medieval outer garment. Women's were floor-length; men's ranged from mid-thigh to ankle.

Cotter: a poor villager, usually holding five acres or less. He had to work for wealthier villages to make ends meet.

Cresset: a bowl of oil with a floating wick used as a lamp.

Cyueles: deep-fried fritters made of a paste of breadcrumbs, ground almonds, eggs, sugar, and salt.

Daub: a clay and plaster mix, reinforced with horsehair and straw, used to plaster the exterior of a house or create interior walls.

Deodand: an object which caused a death. The item was sold and the price given to the king.

Dexter: a war horse, larger than a palfrey or runcie. Also the right-hand direction.

Dibble stick: a stick used to penetrate the soil in planting peas and beans.

Dortoir: the monastery dormitory.

Dower: the groom's financial contribution to marriage, designated for the bride's support during marriage and possible widowhood.

Eels in bruit: eels served in a sauce of white wine, breadcrumbs, onions, and spices.

Farrier: a smith who specialized in shoeing horses.

Fast day: Wednesday, Friday, and Saturday. Not fasting in modern terms, when no food is consumed, but days when no meat, eggs, or animal products were eaten. Fish was on the menu for those who could afford it.

Feverfew: an herb used to reduce fevers.

Flags: flat stones used as paving.

Fraunt hemelle: an egg, meat, and breadcrumb pudding, with pepper and cloves added.

Garderobe: the toilet.

Gathering: eight leaves of parchment, made by folding a prepared hide three times.

Groom: a lower-ranking servant to a lord. Often a teenaged youth ranking above a page and below a valet.

Hall: the largest room in a castle or manor house.

Hamsoken: breaking and entering.

Hanoney: eggs scrambled with onions, and fried.

Heriot: an inheritance tax paid by an heir to a lord, usually the deceased's best animal.

King's Eyre: a royal circuit court generally presided over by a traveling judge.

Kirtle: the basic medieval undershirt.

Let lardes: a custard of eggs, milk, pork fat, parsley, and salt.

Lettuce: wild lettuce and the dried sap was a potent sedative, especially when the plant had gone to seed.

Lychgate: a roofed gate in the churchyard wall under which the deceased rested during the initial part of a funeral.

Marshalsea: the stables and associated accoutrements.

Martinmas: November 11. The traditional date to slaughter animals for winter food.

Maslin: bread made from a mixture of grains; commonly wheat or barley with rye.

Misericord: the rule of St. Benedict prohibited eating flesh, but in the fourteenth century eating meat was allowed so long as it was consumed in the misericord, not the refectory, and not on fast days.

Monkshood: the ground root of monkshood mixed with oils was rubbed into aching joints. A painkiller, but it is extremely poisonous.

Mortuary: a fee paid to a priest for conducting a funeral service and saying prayers for the deceased.

Mussels in broth: mussels cooked in white wine, breadcrumbs, onions, black pepper, and salt.

Novice: a probationary member of a monastic community. The novice's period of instruction and testing usually lasted for one year.

Page: a young male servant, often a youth learning the arts of chivalry before becoming a squire.

Palfrey: a riding horse with a comfortable gait.

Passing bell: the ringing of the parish church bell to indicate the death of a villager.

Poitiers: a battle in September 1356, in which the French king and a son were captured by England and held for ransom.

Pomme dorryse: "golden apples", meatballs made from ground pork, eggs, currants, flour, parsley, and saffron.

Pottage: anything cooked in one pot, from the meanest oatmeal to a savory stew.

Pottage wastere/pottage of whelks: whelks ground into a thick paste, then boiled with ground almonds, rice flour, and spices. Served cold, sliced.

Precentor: the monastic official who directed the church services.

Ravioles: pastries filled with cheese, beaten eggs, occasionally minced pork or poultry, and spices.

Reivers: Scottish raiders who often pillaged the northern counties of England.

Remove: a course at dinner.

Retrochoir: the area immediately behind the monks' choir, occupied during the canonical hours by the sick and infirm, and also by novices.

Runcie: a common horse of a lower grade than a palfrey, often used to pull wagons and carts.

Sacristy: the room in a church where sacred vessels and vestments are stored.

St. Beornwald's Church: today the Church of St. Mary the Virgin, in the fourteenth century it was dedicated to an obscure Saxon saint said to be enshrined in the church.

Sext: the fourth of the canonical hours, celebrated at midday.

Sexton: a church officer who cares for church property, rings the bell, and digs graves.

Shilling: twelve pence.

Simple: honest and without guile.

Solar: a small private room, more easily heated than the great hall, where lords often preferred to spend time, especially in winter. Usually on an upper floor.

Squire: a young man who served as an assistant to a knight.

Statute of Laborers: following the plague of 1348–49, laborers realized their labor was in short supply and demanded higher wages. In 1351, Parliament set wages at the 1347 level. The statute was generally a failure.

Stockfish: inexpensive fish, usually dried cod or haddock, consumed on fast days by those who could afford it.

Stockfish in bruit: cod or haddock in a sauce of white wine, breadcrumbs, onions, parsley, and spices.

Stone: fourteen pounds.

Tabula: a plank which, when struck, signaled time for dinner in a monastery.

Tenant: a free peasant who rented land from a lord. He could pay his rent in labor or, more likely by the fourteenth century, in cash.

Terce: part of the Divine Office, said during the third hour of the day.

Toft: the land surrounding a house, often used for growing vegetables in the medieval period.

Trencher: a large platter, usually made of wood, for serving food.

Trencherman: someone who eats heartily.

Twelfth Night: the evening of January 5, preceding Epiphany.

Valet: a high-ranking servant to a lord. A chamberlain, for example.

Verjure: the tart juice of crushed crab apples.

Viand de leach: a custard made with white wine, beaten egg yolks, full-cream milk, ale, sugar or honey, and spices.

Vicar: a priest serving a parish but, unlike a rector, not entitled to its tithes.

Villein: a non-free peasant. He could not leave his land or service to his lord, or sell animals without permission. But if he could escape his manor for a year and a day, he would be free.

Void: dessert, often sugared fruit and sweetened wine.

Wattle: interlacing sticks used as a foundation and support for daub in building the walls of a house.

Week-work: the two or three days of labor per week (more during harvest) owed by a villein to his lord.

Woad: a plant whose leaves produced a blue dye.

Yardland: about thirty acres. Also called a virgate and in northern England an oxgang.

Dramatis personae

Hugh de Singleton	surgeon, bailiff to Lord Gilbert, and sleuth
Lady Katherine (Kate)	Hugh de Singleton's wife
Bessie, John, and Gilbert	Hugh and Kate's children
Gilbert, Third Baron Talbot	Lord of Bampton Manor
Lady Joan	Lord Gilbert's new wife
Charles de Burgh	Lord Gilbert's nephew
Father Thomas, Father Ralph, and Father Robert	priests at St. Beornwald's Church
Gerard, Martyn, and Piers	clerks to the priests of St. Beornwald's
Andrew Pimm	sexton at St. Beornwald's
Janyn Wagge	large youth newly married to Adela, son of Arthur Wagge (Arthur, now deceased, was Hugh's aide and companion)
Adela Wagge	Kate's former servant and Janyn Wagge's new bride
Maurice Motherby	field worker
Stephen Parkin	Adela's father
Sir Jaket Bec	household knight to Lord Gilbert
Thomas	Sir Jaket's squire
Uctred	an elderly and loyal assistant to Hugh
Will Shillside	coroner of Bampton
Kendrick Wroe	son of Watkin and Maud
John Whitestaff	Bampton's beadle
John Prudhomme	Bampton's reeve

William Lacy	friend of Kendrick and Thomas
Philip Lacy	poor cotter, married to Margery, father of William
Thomas Rous	friend of William and Kendrick

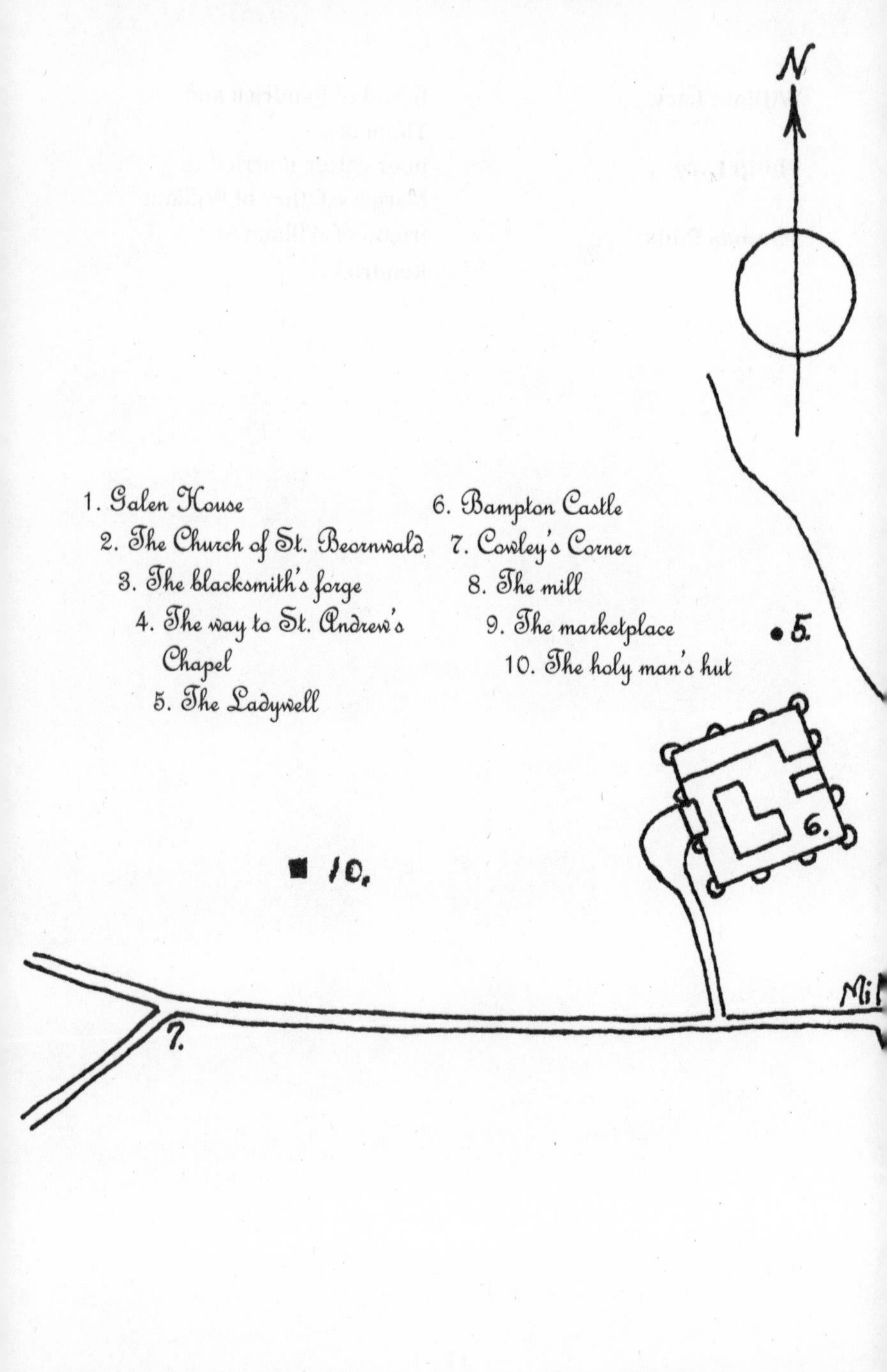
N
1. Galen House
2. The Church of St. Beornwald
3. The blacksmith's forge
4. The way to St. Andrew's Chapel
5. The Ladywell
6. Bampton Castle
7. Cowley's Corner
8. The mill
9. The marketplace
10. The holy man's hut
5.
6.
10.
7.

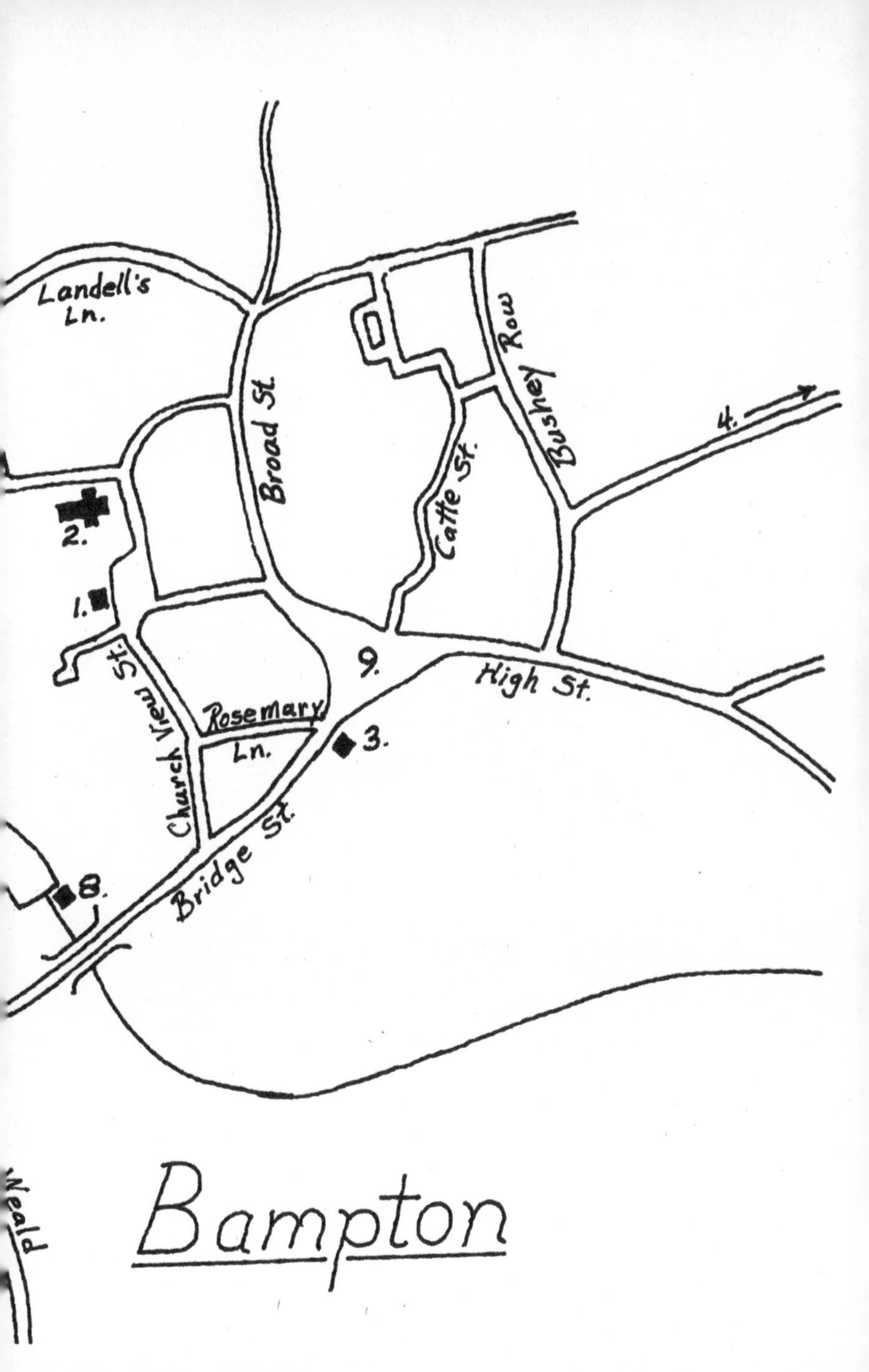
Landell's Ln.
Broad St.
Bushey Row
4.
Catte St.
2.
1.
9.
High St.
Church View St.
Rosemary Ln.
3.
Bridge St.
8.
Bampton

Chapter 1

Kate was correct; I should not have been surprised. She usually is. As my wife predicted, the banns were read for three consecutive Sundays at St. Beornwald's Church in September of the year of our Lord 1377, and early in October, Janyn Wagge wed Adela Parkin in the church porch.

Janyn served Lord Gilbert as a groom at Bampton Castle, assisting the castle farrier in the marshalsea, and Adela, formerly Kate's servant, was employed as assistant in the bakehouse. This arrangement did not endure for many months. By the spring of 1378, Adela was with child, and Lady Joan, Lord Gilbert's new wife, thought it meet that she and Janyn should have a domicile of their own.

Such a residence was available. Walter Maw, Bampton's smith, had died only a few weeks after Janyn and Adela wed. His smithy had been cold for several months and his home empty, as Walter was a widower. His wife had perished, as had many others, when plague returned in 1361, and the smith had not taken another wife.

Janyn's blacksmithing skills were limited. His work with the castle farrier involved shoeing horses but rarely any other work, save for the making or repair of the occasional hinge. Nevertheless, Janyn approached Lord Gilbert about the available tenancy of Walter's house and smithy. This Lord Gilbert was pleased to grant, as Janyn's possession of the place would mean an income, and Lord Gilbert – as most folk knew, although none spoke of it – was something of a spendthrift and perpetually in debt. As a groom, Janyn received coin from Lord Gilbert. As a tenant, the pence would flow the other way.

So the year of our Lord 1378 passed calmly – but for the divided papacy. Urban VI was proclaimed Bishop of Rome in 1378, and all England swore allegiance to him, whilst Clement VII ruled in Avignon, and Scotland followed him. Here was another reason for discord with the Scots. Whatever England did, the Scots would do the opposite. This difference in matters spiritual had already caused temporal disagreement, and reivers saw the conflict as an excuse to raid Northumbria. I was pleased to live far to the south of the Scots border, where no raider, be he ever so bold, would dare hazard an attack.

The division in Holy Mother Church did not seem to trouble the vicars of St. Beornwald's Church. Father Thomas, Father Ralph, and Father Robert continued their duties untroubled by matters in Rome and Avignon. Father Robert, I am sorry to relate, did so with a pronounced limp. The blow to his skull he had received whilst the matter of stolen holy water was under investigation not long ago had permanently affected his gait. I did what I could to repair his broken head, but his limp has not improved for many months. I fear it never will. The priest seems content with this and, when I see him, will often thank me for saving his life, which I probably did.

Friday morning, February 5, three days after Candlemas, about the second hour, I heard the passing bell ring from the tower of St. Beornwald's Church. There was nothing unusual about that. Many folk perish in winter, especially the elderly. I would learn soon enough who had died in Bampton. Sooner than I thought.

Will Shillside, Bampton's coroner, thumped upon the door of Galen House a short time later. He told me he had been called to assemble his jury to inspect a corpse found encrusted in the icy fringe of Shill Brook, a short distance north of the mill. Here was the reason for the passing bell. "Death by misadventure" was the jury's conclusion. When the corpse was drawn from the stream, no evidence of homicide was found. And who would slay a lad of thirteen years? The remains were those of Kendrick Wroe, whose parents, Maud and Watkin, did not know he was missing until they found his bed cold Friday morning. So they said.

This discovery was no responsibility of mine. I am a surgeon. I deal with the complaints of the living. The dead are the concern of St. Beornwald's vicars. But as Bampton's bailiff, Will thought I should know. I was saddened to hear that a lad not much more advanced in years than our eldest son, John, had perished in such tragic circumstances. A life cut short in its prime.

Two members of the coroner's jury had dragged Kendrick's corpse from the brook, placed it upon a pallet, and carried it to his parents' home. The lad had been found in a stream, but must be washed before burial, as custom requires. And there would be a wake. A costly affair for tenants, but again, custom requires such, and neighbors would gossip for months about the lack of respect shown by Watkin and Maud for their deceased son should they not at least provide a few ewers of ale to mourners. And Watkin and Maud are not poor.

I did wonder what a lad might be doing that would cause him to tumble into the cold water of Shill Brook.

'Twould have been understandable if he had done so in July. It was likely he and his friends had intentionally done so in the warmer months, and as often clambered out. At the place where Kendrick's corpse was found, the brook is little more than knee deep. Why did the lad not scramble out? Was he overcome by the cold water?

Many questions came to mind, but as the lad was dead he could not answer them, and death by misadventure did not require the attention of a bailiff. There would be no deodand, of course. How could one sell Shill Brook and send the coins to the king? Nor would Lord Gilbert be able to claim a heriot, as Kendrick was but a lad. No deodand, no heriot. With these absent, I had no obligation. So I thought.

Kendrick's younger brother, Alward, a lad of ten years or so, banged upon the door of Galen House shortly after dinner. His mother, he said, begged me to attend her. The Wroes live on Bushy Row, in a substantial two-bay house, which Watkin could afford as he rented a full yardland from Lord Gilbert.

I made my way to Bushy Row, curious about the summons. When I arrived at the Wroe house I found Maud and a neighbor, Alyce Hoppe, drying Kendrick's corpse after washing, preparing to clothe the body before folk arrived for the wake.

Maud heard me rap upon her door and opened it, but did not offer me a "good day". Why would she? Her eldest son, I saw, lay upon a table, swathed in linen drying strips.

"How may I serve you?" I said. I also omitted "good day", as it was surely not. "Alward said you desired my presence."

"Aye. We was washin' Kendrick, me an' Alyce, an' we seen somethin' we don't understand. Come an' see."

The woman led me to the table upon which Kendrick lay, and lifted his arm. "Look there," she said, and pointed to his armpit.

I saw immediately what had caught her attention. Had the lad been a few years older and hirsute, the foliage which sprouts from under a grown man's armpits would have obscured the wound. For wound it likely was.

I bent closer to obtain a better view of the small gash. 'Twas no longer than the width of my index fingernail. If the cut had bled, the water of Shill Brook had washed away the evidence.

"Has Kendrick complained of injuring himself recently?" I asked.

"Nay," Maud replied.

"Where is his kirtle? And cotehardie?"

Maud produced the garments, and I saw small punctures in the linen and wool which corresponded with the cut in Kendrick's armpit.

"'Tis my understanding," I said, "that when you arose this morning, Kendrick was already away. Did he often arise before dawn?"

It seemed odd to me that a lad would choose to leave his warm bed on a cold winter's morning before he was required to do so. And the winter of 1379 was unusually cold. Plowing usually begins at Candlemas, and so it did this year, but the frost was only recently gone from the soil, and nights were so cold that a skim of ice would form on the mill pond and the weedy fringes of the brook.

"Not often," Maud said. She seemed reluctant to answer. "Most days 'e was slug-a-bed."

Like most lads, I thought. "When he did rise early from his bed, did he give reason why?"

"Just said 'e couldn't sleep."

This was no good reason for leaving a warm bed on a cold morning. I was becoming suspicious of Kendrick's reason for rising before dawn. This is an occupational hazard. Bailiffs are, by nature, suspicious. Those who are gullible soon lose their post.

I am Hugh de Singleton, surgeon, educated at Oxford and Paris, and employed as bailiff to Lord Gilbert, Third Baron Talbot, at his manor of Bampton. Maud Wroe had called me to examine her son for two reasons. As surgeon I could likely identify the cut in Kendrick's armpit, and as bailiff I might discover who – or *what* – had made the wound.

If Kendrick Wroe had reasons for rising early, of which his parents knew not – or even if they did and Maud was not willing to say – I knew of a man who might have observed the youth whilst he prowled the town before dawn.

Bampton's holy man often walked the streets after curfew. John Whitestaff, Bampton's beadle, knew of the holy man's custom and did not accost him if he saw him. I had told John to ignore the holy man if he found him about in the night after curfew. The holy man was a second pair of eyes for me, and could tell me of nocturnal events which had occurred whilst I slept.

The holy man had first appeared in Bampton nearly six years past. He sat at the corner of Church View Street and Bridge Street, and when children passed he rose, placed hands upon their heads, and mouthed a silent blessing. This strange man, behaving strangely, had caught my attention. I felt he might require my vigilance.

I discovered he had found shelter in an abandoned swineherd's hut but a hundred or so paces from Cowley's Corner, to the west of the castle. I had followed him there and questioned him about his presence in Bampton. This was an arduous business, for the holy man never spoke. He answered my questions only with a nod or a shake of the head. I eventually learned why.

He had gone on pilgrimage to Compostela, but lost his way and wandered into Grenada, where Mussulmen enslaved him. When he would not be persuaded to accept Mohammed's teachings, his tongue was torn from his mouth for his heresy. After some months he escaped his captors and made his way back to England. He attempted to join some monastery as a lay brother, but due to his deformity none would have him. He wandered the realm, seeking sustenance and shelter wherever it might be found, until he came to Bampton, where he found agreeable folk who, in return for his blessings upon their children, would give him the occasional sack of peas or barley or an egg.

A few years past, the holy man had aided me in capturing a felon, and for this assistance Lord Gilbert had the crumbling swineherd's hut demolished and a new shelter erected in its place, with sturdy walls of wattle and daub, a well-thatched roof, and a hearthstone in the middle where the holy man might simmer his pottage and warm himself on cold winter days. Such as this day.

The holy man's door was shut against the cold. I rapped upon the sturdy portal and called out my name. He had been tending a kettle of peas pottage bubbling upon the hearthstone. Smoke from the smoldering coals rose to the eave vents. The holy man tugged a forelock and pointed to his bench, which he had drawn close to the hearthstone, then sat at one end whilst I took the other.

The holy man never begins a conversation. A man who cannot – or will not – speak must await the voice of his caller.

"Have you heard of the death of Kendrick Wroe?" I began.

The holy man shook his head, and his eyes seemed to widen. Had the news shocked him?

"Do you know who Kendrick is . . . *was*?"

He nodded.

"The lad was found this morning, cold and lifeless, in Shill Brook. He evidently left his home before dawn and had done so other times. Have you seen him about the town in the night?"

The holy man shook his head.

I wished the answer to that question was otherwise, but was not surprised at his response. Folk of Bampton have learned that the holy man is often found on the streets after curfew, with my knowledge and permission, so if they are about some tenebrous activity and do not want to be discovered, they know they should watch for and avoid the holy man. And, according to Maud, Kendrick had left his bed just before dawn, whereas the holy man was most likely to observe the darkened streets before midnight, or not long after.

My hope that the holy man could tell me something of Kendrick Wroe's nocturnal activity was dashed. This was a fairly normal occurrence. Rarely do my desires conform to unfolding events. Why should they? Why should I be unlike other men, whose schemes oft go awry?

The poor young lad's death remained a mystery; one that I was obliged to solve. Who could possibly wish to murder a boy of thirteen? It made no sense to me.

Chapter 2

Darkness and Kendrick's wake came early. We were yet six weeks or so 'til equinox, and a like time past the shortest day of the year. Roger Bacon said the calendar was out of joint, and his argument was persuasive. But most folk care little. They rise with the sun and take to their beds when it sets. What more do they need to know?

Bessie was old enough to watch over John and Gilbert, although John was convinced he needed no looking after. Kate put Gilbert to bed, admonished John that he was to obey his sister, then joined me for the short walk to Bushy Row. Bessie was instructed to bar the door of Galen House when we departed, and I heard it fall into place as we set forth. When most folk are attending a wake, others may decide 'tis a suitable time to do hamsoken.

Maud and Watkin had purchased fresh ale from Milicent Baker, Bampton's most respected ale wife. They also provided maslin loaves, although there was no butter or cheese, as this was a fast day.

When I left Maud and Alyce earlier that day, I had made no public determination as to the cause of Kendrick's death. So far as the women knew, the cut under Kendrick's armpit and the tiny slit in his kirtle and cotehardie were coincidental to his death in the frigid water of Shill Brook. But bailiffs do not believe in coincidence.

As I thought on the matter during the day, I became convinced that young Kendrick had not died due to falling into a cold stream. Someone, I suspected, had plunged a thin dagger between the lad's ribs, then placed the corpse into Shill Brook to cover his tracks. Or mayhap Kendrick had tried to cross the brook to escape his assailant and perished there.

Why would some man do this, and to such a young lad? I resolved to seek Will Shillside after Kendrick's funeral and find the place along the brook where Kendrick's corpse had been found. As all considered the death the result of misadventure, no one had thought to examine the brook and its banks for evidence of murder.

Next day, I heard the funeral procession approach long before it came to Church View Street and past Galen House. Female mourners, friends of Maud, set up a howl as they walked behind the coffin. Watkin and three other men carried the box which held Kendrick's corpse. They, in contrast to the women, walked silently with a slow, measured tread.

The bearers set the coffin down under the lychgate and Father Robert spoke a prayer for Kendrick's soul, that he might be speedily released from purgatory – if there is such a place. Which is not to say that Father Robert questions the existence of purgatory. Such doubts are my own. Mortuary fees and priestly income would be much reduced were my views adopted by most folks, so I keep them to myself. Bailiffs find enough enemies without inviting more.

Father Robert spoke the homily at the funeral mass, which was much like other funeral sermons I have heard: to whit, we must all be ready to meet the Lord Christ, for no man knows when he will be required to do so. Witness the youth of Kendrick Wroe. When he took to his bed

Thursday evening, he could not have known 'twas the last time he would do so.

The coffin was taken from the lychgate to the churchyard, where Father Robert sprinkled holy water on the place where Kendrick would rest until the Lord Christ returned. Then the sexton, Andrew Pimm, and an assistant began to dig the grave.

Pimm halted the excavation when the grave was little more than waist deep. Folk have been buried in St. Beornwald's churchyard for hundreds of years, their graves unmarked and forgotten. Dig too deep and their bones might be uncovered.

The coffin lid was not fixed in place, as the box was merely rented from Andrew Carpenter. Only the wealthy would consider burying a family member in an expensive wooden coffin. This coffin had likely been carried to the churchyard many times, and would be again, until some prosperous villager decided to honor a family member by entombing them in a wooden coffin. What difference this would make to the dead, I cannot guess. For my part, should I die before Kate, I hope she will put me in the churchyard wrapped only in a shroud. Wool or linen is less dear than wood. The coins she might spend for a coffin would be more useful to her and Bessie and John and Gilbert than to me.

I stopped Will Shillside as he passed through the lychgate after the funeral and asked that he show me where Kendrick's corpse was discovered.

We trudged across the meadow to the west of the church. The place where Kendrick was found was level with the church, about a hundred paces from where the flow slowed and broadened into the mill pond.

"Who found the lad?" I asked.

"'Twas Maurice Motherby who told me of the death."

"Was he troubled about the discovery?"

"Aye. Who wouldn't be?"

"Indeed. The death of a child is a terrible thing. Did he say what brought him to the brook so early in the day?"

"Nay. Told me of the dead lad, that's all."

Whatever reason Maurice may have had for walking the bank of Shill Brook, it did not seem likely to me that it was he who had thrust a slender dagger between Kendrick's ribs. Had he done so, why would he lead Will to the place where he had done murder? He would have wanted to be thought far from the scene.

Brown winter grass and sedge was trampled and broken where Will and his coroner's jury had pulled Kendrick from the icy grip of the brook. The past winter had been so cold that the mill pond had briefly frozen over, and only the middle of Shill Brook had no fringe of ice. The days were beginning to warm, but the nights remained cold enough that the margins of the stream had retained some ice.

From the place of trampled grass and sedge I scanned the far bank, some four or five paces distant, then began a slow walk south, toward the mill pond, looking for I knew not what, but ready to recognize it when I saw it. Something foreign to a brook and its banks in the winter, I supposed.

I arrived at the pond, with Will following close behind. He knew from my actions that I sought something, and at the pond he asked me. "What we lookin' for?" he said, including himself in the search.

"Anything out of place," I said, and turned to retrace my steps. I went past the place where Kendrick's body was found, slowed my progress, and twenty or so paces to the north found what I sought. More or less.

A net could not, I suppose, accurately be described as "out of place" when found alongside a body of water. The net was crude, fashioned from strands of a hempen rope which had been unraveled. The mesh was not tight. Small fish could escape the web. But then who would cast a net into a stream or pond intent on catching small fish?

Stones had been tied to one side of the net, to weight it so that it would sink rapidly to the stream bed and capture any unwary pike or trout. Whoso had made this net would not limit his diet on fast days to peas and beans and such, as most of the poorer folk of Bampton were inclined to do.

The net measured about three paces square, and seemed quite new. I saw no repairs where it might have snagged upon rocks or sunken sticks and the like. Why had it been left here? Someone had gone to much trouble to make this net. 'Twas surely too valuable to discard. Unless it was no longer useful to whoso crafted it. Was this Kendrick Wroe's work? This seemed credible.

Was Kendrick caught unawares whilst using the net to poach Lord Gilbert's fish? Such an apprehension was my duty, and until this minute I had known nothing of anyone taking fish from Shill Brook.

"That net belonged to Kendrick, you think?" Will said, interrupting my thoughts.

"Aye. Tell no one of this discovery. A murder has been committed, and I do not want the felon to know that I suspect it so. Most folk believe Kendrick perished because he tumbled into a cold stream. I want the slayer to think he has succeeded in covering his tracks. He may then become careless in his words and deeds."

"You think the Wroe lad was surprised while catchin' fish from the brook? Why would that cause a man to slay 'im?"

"That is what I must discover. Remember, tell no one of this."

Will nodded.

It has long been my practice to record felonious incidents I am required to untangle. I have a gathering of parchment at Galen House, but may require more. This would entail a journey to Oxford and a visit to a stationer's shop. But I will not need to purchase ink.

I first met Kate when I visited her father's stationer's shop in Oxford. She made ink, which was sold in his shop. Last autumn I collected a sack of oak galls, which Kate soaked in rainwater by the kitchen fire. Then she mixed sulphur into water and added a few bits of cast-off iron from Janyn's forge. This produced copperas, which Kate then mixed with the oak gall solution, then added ground gum arabic to thicken the blend.

So I was well equipped to record the solution to young Kendrick Wroe's death. All I needed to do was solve the slaying. The writing would be easier than the doing.

I freed the stones which had been used to weight the net, then wrapped the hempen cords about my elbow. 'Twould be good, I thought, to keep the net at hand. Perhaps I might find the rope from which the strands had been unraveled. Although one hempen rope is much like another.

Dinner at Galen House was more palatable than usual for a fast day. Kate had prepared pottage wastere. Such a meal was as succulent as Lord Gilbert would enjoy in his hall this day. It had been prepared with Bessie's help. When Adela wed Janyn and left our employ, Kate decided not to hire another servant, but rather to teach Bessie the homely skills she would need as a wife. Some day. Not too soon, I hoped.

But Kate's opinion on the matter was surely sound. Bessie was unlikely to wed a noble spouse and have servants to wait upon her. Although such a thing is possible, I suppose. I am now Sir Hugh, since Edward of Woodstock granted me a knighthood nine years past. Which means my wife is Lady Katherine, and Bessie is properly addressed as Lady Elizabeth.

The thought of Lord Gilbert at his dinner caused me to modify my plans for the afternoon. Lord Gilbert wants to be kept informed of events on his manor. I had intended to visit Maurice Motherby, but he could wait. A homicide which had occurred only a few hundred paces from the castle would require prompt telling. Lord Gilbert had surely heard of Kendrick's death, but like others would likely have assumed the coroner's jury to be correct in assigning the cause to immersion in freezing water.

A blazing fire warmed the solar where I found Lord Gilbert and his wife, Lady Joan, daughter of the Earl of Stafford and widow of John Charleton, Third Baron Charleton.

"Sir Hugh, I give you good day. How may I serve you?" Such a greeting was mere formality. All know that a bailiff, even one knighted by Edward of Woodstock, serves his lord and not the other way round.

Lord Gilbert's new spouse gazed at me down the length of her long, sharp nose. Her mouth, whenever I saw her, seemed perpetually pursed, as if she had just had a swallow of verjuice, and her arms were crossed in what could be considered an expression of disapproval. 'Tis said that Lady Joan brought with her to Bampton Castle a considerable legacy from Sir John. This is not declared in public. But Lord Gilbert did not wed the lady for her beauty or scintillating wit. What other reason could there be?

"I bring you a report of murder," I said.

"Who is slain?" Lord Gilbert said.

"The lad, Kendrick Wroe."

"He who was found frozen in Shill Brook? He died of the cold, did he not?"

"Mayhap the cold water played some part in his death, but he was also stabbed."

"Was the wound not visible to Will Shillside and his coroner's jury?"

"Nay. 'Twas only when the corpse was bathed for burial that it was discovered. Some man pierced him to the heart with a thin blade. The stroke was delivered under his armpit, as if he had raised his arms to defend himself."

"Why would some rogue do so? Had the lad made enemies?"

"One, at least. A short distance from where Kendrick died, I found a crude net, made from unraveled hempen rope."

Lord Gilbert frowned as the import of my words struck him. "A poacher? Taking fish from Shill Brook? Was the lad slain because he witnessed this and could identify the miscreant?"

"Mayhap. But 'tis my belief young Kendrick himself was the poacher."

"Hmm. Then why should some man slay him?"

"If my hunch is correct, the murder makes no sense. Will told me Maurice Motherby found Kendrick dead and reported it to him."

"What was Maurice doing prowling the bank of Shill Brook at dawn? Are you sure he was not the poacher and slew the lad for discovering him?"

"I am not sure of anything, but would a man commit murder, then lead others to his victim?"

"Ah . . . I see your point."

"And besides, Will imparted to me that Maurice appeared to be in a state of great distress at having happened upon the poor lad's body. I'm going from here to speak to him. Perhaps after I have done so I will know more of this sorry business."

"When you do, tell me straight away."

Throughout this conversation Lady Joan's head had swiveled from me to Lord Gilbert, a disdainful scowl creasing her forehead whenever her gaze fell upon me. Some folk can put others in their place without a word. Lady Joan is one of these.

Chapter 3

Plowing for the new season begins at Candlemas, no matter how miserable the weather. Frost was out of the ground, so men were at work in their strips turning the soil. I found Maurice Motherby guiding a team of oxen whilst his companion wrestled with the plow handles.

I waited at the road until Maurice approached, then waved to him to halt the beasts and draw near. Most men are not eager to greet their bailiff, especially when it is he seeking them rather than the other way round.

"I give you good day," I smiled, attempting to put the man at ease. Had I thought him guilty of Kendrick's murder I would rather have had him apprehensive. A malefactor will sometimes reveal his guilt through facial expressions and shifting eyes. I saw no such reaction with Maurice. "Will Shillside told me 'twas you who notified him about finding Kendrick Wroe dead in Shill Brook yesterday morn. Describe to me exactly what you saw."

Maurice tugged a forelock and began to speak. "Was just comin' daylight when I seen 'im. Half in, half out the water, 'e was, poor little lad." His voice trembled slightly.

"As if he was trying to scramble out of the water when he died?" I said.

"Aye. Just so. I left off me business an' went to Will straight away."

"What was the business you were about?" I asked casually, not wishing to alarm Maurice by showing overmuch interest in his activities.

"Goin' to the forest to gather wood for me hearth. Been so cold that what I collected for winter's 'bout gone. Thought to walk north 'til the brook got small enough I could jump over an' get to the forest that way."

This made sense. The winter had been long and harsh. Tenants and villeins did have permission to take fallen branches from Lord Gilbert's forest, and a hundred or so paces to the north of where Kendrick's corpse was found, Shill Brook shrank to leapable size.

"Did you return to the brook to resume your intended business after seeking Will?"

"Nay. Still need to do so. By the time I shown Will where Kendrick was, 'twas time to begin the day's plowin'."

"You did not walk north along the brook after finding the corpse?"

"Nay."

I decided not to mention the crude net I had found. If Maurice had not walked north along the brook, he would not have seen it. And as the hempen cords were brown like the sedge grass and vegetation, I had nearly missed seeing the net myself as it lay amongst the verdure.

Maurice fidgeted, and looked to the oxen and his plow partner. He wished to be at his work. Two men with a team of four oxen might expect to plow an acre each day. My questions had interrupted Maurice's work and put him off his schedule.

I bade the man good day. He went back to his goad stick and I to the opening in the hedge which gave onto the road. As my feet found the rutted surface, I casually glanced back to see how Maurice fared as he and his plow partner began a new furrow. I was surprised to see that they had not begun. The oxen stood placidly, and the two men stood beside the plow in conversation.

As I watched, Maurice spoke but I was too far away to hear his words. He turned toward me and I saw that his face was creased with a smile. This vanished like dew in the summer sun, and he trotted over to the lead oxen. His plow mate also turned toward me, saw me looking back, and hurried to his place at the plowshares. Maurice urged the oxen into motion and the plow began a new furrow.

When Lot's wife turned to look back, she became a pillar of salt. Looking back on Maurice and his companion did not bring the same result to me, but I was left with an uneasy feeling. Did Maurice find humor in the death of Kendrick Wroe? Or was his jocular manner related to some other matter known only to him and his plow partner?

I had discounted Maurice Motherby as a murderer. Did his surreptitious grin mean I should no longer do so? What motive could he have had? None that I could think of. But just because I was unaware of a motive did not mean there wasn't one. 'Twas time to speak to some other lads of Bampton. They might know why Kendrick had left his warm bed before dawn.

At the wake, Maud and Watkin had named several of Kendrick's friends, and I asked which of these their son was most likely to have confided in. They named William Lacy and Thomas Rous.

It was too late in the day to seek William and Thomas. Thick clouds obscured the winter sun. Better to speak to the lads another time. For now I would return to Galen House, a warm supper, a warm bed, and a warm wife.

Kate and Bessie prepared let lardes for Sunday dinner. As usual, Bessie kept the conversation going during the meal, whilst John set to his dinner silently. The lad is not dull - he is learning to read and write English, French, and Latin - but seems to be of the opinion that a meal is meant to be devoured, its purpose subverted by too much discourse.

I have also been teaching Bessie Latin. Kate believes that knowing how to read and write English, and perhaps a bit of French, is enough for any lass, and rolls her eyes when I sit Bessie down at the table to study.

"You intend to make a scholar of her?" Kate grinned one time. "What college in Oxford will admit her? And what swain will court a maid who knows more than he?"

"A lad wise enough to see intelligence as a virtue. And who can tell? Mayhap Bessie will wed a scholar. Not all scholars are bachelors."

As might be expected, conversation drifted during the dinner to the untimely death of Kendrick Wroe. Kate knew of the wound found under the lad's armpit, but Bessie and John did not. So far as they knew, his demise was a useful lesson in avoiding frigid water. Nothing more. But then Bessie said something which arrested my attention.

"Thomas doesn't think Kendrick died of cold."

"Thomas Rous?" I said.

"Aye."

"Did he say why he thought that?"

"He said Kendrick told him he slipped and fell into Shill Brook just before Twelfth Night. Said it woke him but didn't hurt him."

"Did Kendrick tell Thomas what he was doing on the bank of Shill Brook in the dead of winter?"

"Nay. Least, if he did, Thomas didn't tell me."

"Did Kendrick tell Thomas what time of day it was when he fell into the brook?"

"Thomas thought 'twas early morn, else folk would have been about and heard Kendrick shout for help. And Kendrick told Thomas the dunking woke him."

"Hmm. Must have been early if the dunking woke him. Mayhap he did not shout for help because he needed none."

"Or," Bessie said slyly, "he wanted no one to know he was prowling along Shill Brook at such an early hour."

"What is your opinion? You know . . . *knew* Kendrick."

"Not well," Bessie said. "Kept to himself, did Kendrick. Seemed shy when in the presence of his bailiff's daughter," she laughed.

This, I admit, pleased me. Bessie takes after her mother, and lacks my long nose and somewhat irregular features. My Kate is a beauty, whose features time has not ravaged. Bessie is beginning to attract second glances from the village lads. And I have observed Charles de Burgh, Lord Gilbert's nephew and page, taking notice of her.

"Has Thomas said much about Kendrick's death?" I asked.

"Nay. Oddly, though, he seems not much surprised."

Kendrick was past the age of death from childhood diseases. By the time a lad or lass is ten years of age they have either succumbed to illness or survived the maladies of tender years. So why would Thomas Rous be unsurprised about Kendrick's death when he had prevailed over the ailments of childhood?

Perhaps Thomas's attitude was of no import. Or mayhap Bessie had misread his demeanor. But I didn't believe it so. Bessie is a perceptive lass. If she thought Thomas had expected some misfortune to befall Kendrick, it was likely the Rous lad was as observant as Bessie thought.

What was Kendrick in the habit of doing which caused Thomas to expect calamity? Did Thomas know that Kendrick sometimes left his bed before dawn and walked the banks of Shill Brook with a crude net, intent on poaching Lord Gilbert's fish? Was there more to it than the simple matter of stealing a fish or two to supplement his family's meager meals?

If Thomas knew of this practice of Kendrick's, what would prevent him from trying the same activity? Thomas was a year older than Kendrick. A year taller, a year heavier, a year stronger. Might he and Kendrick have quarreled there on the banks of Shill Brook, and Thomas pierced Kendrick with a thin blade? Perhaps Kendrick had wanted all of the pickings for himself. I supposed the fatal stroke could have been accidental - Kendrick turning from the stroke, arms raised to defend himself. Of course, this could have been the circumstance no matter who had delivered the killing thrust. Then again, perhaps Thomas was aware of a threat to Kendrick's life entirely unconnected to the brook's aquatic inhabitants.

And what of William Lacy? Had Kendrick, in a moment of youthful boasting, told William of his success at capturing fish for his parents' fast-day meals? I had my doubts. If Kendrick had done so, would William admit it? So far as I knew, most folk yet thought Kendrick dead of immersion in a frozen stream. If William knew of Kendrick's poaching, he might be wise enough to keep the knowledge to himself. To admit that he knew what Kendrick was doing might be to implicate himself in a felony, particularly if Kendrick had been supplying others with pike and trout for a small amount of coin. Or mayhap

Kendrick had been involved in a more sinister scheme that I yet knew nothing about.

William Lacy's parents resided in the Weald, and were tenants of the Bishop of Exeter. I had, therefore, no authority over them or their children. Nevertheless, Lord Gilbert's proximity at Bampton Castle provided influence where none might be expected or asserted. If I asked questions of William Lacy or his parents I might, therefore, expect some degree of cooperation.

Tenants of the bishop in the Weald are somewhat less prosperous than Lord Gilbert's tenants in Bampton. Most survive on half a yardland or less, and so hire themselves out at planting and harvest to more affluent neighbors. The house of Philip and Margery Lacy was a single bay and badly in need of thatching. A heavy rain would likely soak the souls under such a roof. Folk who lived in a house like this would not dine upon fish on fast days, but on pea or oat or barley pottage. Unless they could obtain fish from Shill Brook with a net, either directly or indirectly.

Monday dawned warmer than past days. No ice would form on the banks of the mill pond or wrap the mill wheel. Warmer, aye, but not warm, so the flimsy door to the Lacy hut was shut against the cold when I rapped upon it. The door rattled upon leather hinges, and a moment later I heard the bar lift.

Philip Lacy peered at me through the partially open door, recognized me, then opened it wide and tugged a forelock. Well he might. This was surely the first time a man knighted by Edward of Woodstock had appeared at his door.

A puff of smoke wafted through the open door. The thatching over the eave vents had evidently collapsed, so the fumes from the hearthstone had no means of escape but through the door. Philip's unkempt hair and beard were wreathed in smoke. He coughed, but did not invite me in. I would not have entered if he had. My cotehardie would have reeked for a week had I done so.

I saw three small faces appear behind Philip; children curious to see who was calling so early on a chilly morning. One of these faces was surely William's. I asked.

Philip turned and motioned to the eldest of the children to approach. "What you want with William?" he said hesitantly.

"A friend of his recently perished. I wish to speak to him of the death."

"Kendrick? Stupid lad, fallin' into icy water an' not the sense to draw hisself out. What d'you need to know from William?"

"That is a matter I will discuss with the lad."

I could see Philip's mind was at work by the expression on his face. Should he permit Lord Gilbert's bailiff, who had no authority in the Weald, to speak privily to his son? Apparently, he decided there was nothing to be gained by forbidding this, so acquiesced. "William, Lord Gilbert's bailiff would speak to you."

A small lad crept past his father, shyly emulating his father by tugging a forelock, then stood silently before me.

"Will, is it?" I said. "Come walk with me and speak of Kendrick Wroe."

The lad looked to his father, as if seeking permission. He received a slight nod, then followed me to the path which led between the houses of the Weald.

William was a slight lad, mayhap a year younger than Kendrick, and weighing no more than six stone, if that. In a quarrel with Kendrick or Thomas Rous, he would have come off much the worse. Unless he'd had a dagger, that was. But where would a poor cotter's son find such a weapon? William seemed too timorous to strike anyone, yet even the fainthearted will, I think, react to an affront if goaded.

"I am told that you and Kendrick were friends," I began.

William made no reply, evidently believing that silence conferred assent.

"When did you last speak to him?"

The lad screwed up his face, as if trying to recall. "Thursday," he finally said.

"Of what did you speak?"

"Plowin' an' such."

"Is your father part of a plow team?"

"Nay," the lad snorted. "Got no oxen, 'ave we! 'E 'ires out to them as got oxen an' strips."

"And then pays to have his own strips plowed?"

"Aye," William agreed.

"What else did Kendrick speak of? Did he tell you he planned to spend time at Shill Brook next day?"

"Nay. Why would 'e? No reason to go there this time o' year."

"You and other lads would sport in the brook on hot summer days?" I asked.

"Aye."

"Then you were surprised when you learned that Kendrick had died in the brook?"

"Aye."

Had there been a brief hesitation before Will's reply? Probably my imagination.

We came to the end of the lane, where the Weald had come by its name, the habitations ended, and a few acres of forest – also the possession of the Bishop of Exeter – began.

The return to William's home was silent until we were but a few paces from the house.

"Thought Kendrick was smart enough to stay clear of Shill Brook," he said. "Cold as it's been. Must have seen summat of interest what kept drawin' 'im back there."

I wondered what that something might have been. Had the Wroe family been so desperate to supplement their income that Kendrick had felt it his duty to poach fish from the brook? I suspected not. In which case there had to be another reason for his presence there that day.

Philip Lacy stood at the door to his hovel as we came near. Did he appear relieved that I had returned with his eldest child? Had he feared that I would not? Bailiffs to powerful lords are prone to unpredictable behavior. For whatever reason, he again tugged a forelock as William brushed past and entered his home. The door closed after them, and I made my way back to Galen House and my dinner.

Kate and Bessie had prepared arbolettys. As we ate, Bessie spoke again of Kendrick Wroe, and I learned that rumors regarding his death were spreading through Bampton.

"Roger Witherly said he heard his father tell Alan Blake that Kendrick was stabbed," my daughter said. She looked at me, as if awaiting confirmation.

If the cause of Kendrick's death was circulating through the town, what harm could come from my affirming what Bessie had learned? "This is so," I said. "The cold of the stream may have played a part, but he bore a wound where 'twas likely he was pierced."

Gaston Miller would have witnessed the discovery and retrieval of Kendrick Wroe's corpse. After dinner, I sought him at the mill.

The winter had been so cold that often his ice-encrusted wheel would not turn for days at a time, and a layer of ice was occasionally visible upon the wheel in the morning, before Gaston opened the sluice and set the wheel in motion.

I crossed Shill Brook, then took the well-worn, mud-encrusted path to the mill. In February there was little business for Gaston. Folk who wanted their corn ground to flour had the task completed shortly after harvest. If grain was ground in late winter, the work was likely done surreptitiously on some tenant's house at an illegal hand mill. 'Twas my business, as Bampton's bailiff, to root out such forbidden activity. I had better ways to spend my time.

Gaston had installed a hearthstone in one corner of the mill. I found him toasting his feet before a small blaze. When I entered the structure, Gaston lifted his considerable bulk from his bench, tugged a forelock, and asked how he might serve me. He looked nervous and avoided my gaze.

Millers are, as a class, assumed to be dishonest in dealing with their patrons, holding back more than their due to sell for their own profit, or to consume. In Gaston's case, if he kept more flour than was his lawful share, I believe he ate the largesse.

As his bailiff, 'twas my obligation to see that he kept no more than was his legal portion. How to do this without peering over his shoulder with weights and measures, I knew not. And Gaston held back a small enough quantity of flour that he did not raise the ire of townsfolk. Well, not much.

"Friday last, did the mill operate?" I began.

"Nay. None came with corn, so the sluice was closed."

"But you were here when Kendrick Wroe's corpse was drawn from the brook?"

"Aye. Replaced a rotting plank whilst the wheel was still. 'Eard the commotion when Will an' 'is jury 'auled the lad from the water."

"Had you seen Kendrick lurking about near the mill in the past weeks?"

"Nay."

This was to be expected. If Kendrick, fresh from his bed, had prowled the banks of Shill Brook before dawn, neither the miller nor any other man would have seen him. Probably.

"Have you noticed anyone else scouting the banks of the brook?"

"No, but rumor 'as it that some young lady's been spotted in these parts early, like."

This was new information. Who could the young lady be? It was quite unheard of for a woman to be seen wandering alone at the crack of dawn. Could this be true? Or was the miller dissembling, doing all he could to throw me off the scent?

"Do you have any idea who the young lady might be?" I enquired.

"None," said Gaston, looking down at his hands. "Seen you an' the coroner lookin' for somethin' Saturday. You find what you was after?"

I noted the rapid change in conversation. "Not really," I said evasively.

"No net or nothin'?" he probed.

Although the information that Kendrick's death was perhaps a murder and not misadventure was now being bandied about, I did not want folk to know of the net. I had no particular reason to hold back this information, but in past situations I had learned that it was beneficial when seeking a felon to possess knowledge that others had not. Worry about what I knew might keep a miscreant awake at night, or mayhap render him careless. It surprised me that Gaston knew about the net and thought it prudent to mention it to me.

"Why should there have been a net?"

"Folk sayin' 'e were always out poachin' Lord Gilbert's trout."

Another interesting comment. Why should Gaston Miller want me to think badly of Kendrick Wroe? Did he know more about the murder than he was letting on?

"I been hearin' rumors that the lad was slain. No misadventure about it."

Again, I found his curiosity in relation to the information I had gleaned so far intriguing. "Folk will talk," I said nonchalantly.

"Aye. Complainin' 'bout the cold is old, so any new thing gets tongues waggin'."

I had learned what I could from the miller, so bade the man good day. A return visit would almost certainly be in order once I had learned more about the poor lad's death and had a more informed line of questioning in my mind.

Gaston returned to his hearthstone, where the small blaze was nearly extinguished, and I departed the mill. The silent, motionless mill wheel caught my attention, and I saw the new plank which Gaston had nailed in place. Doubtless with nails made by Janyn Wagge.

A thought crossed my mind. The wound under Kendrick's armpit was, I thought, made by a slender dagger. Might a nail make a similar wound? Had Gaston purchased an extra nail to carry out the grisly deed? But what would the miller stand to gain from the child's death?

Janyn's forge was on my way home, just a few paces past the bridge over Shill Brook. I decided to call in and speak with him.

Pounding upon a red-hot iron was an exhausting task on a summer day, but for the past few months Janyn's labor was the only way a man of Bampton could raise a sweat.

Janyn's work was completed for the day, his forge covered and cooling. A door between the shop and house was open, allowing residual heat from the forge to warm the house. I entered the shop and rapped upon the open door.

Adela appeared, her babe upon her hip. "You seek Janyn?" she asked.

"Aye."

Adela turned and called for her husband. He soon appeared. I was again struck by how closely he resembled his father, Arthur, deceased of plague now for several years. Arthur had been brawny, but Janyn's work with hammer and tongs had made him even more so.

He tugged a forelock and spoke. "I give you good day, Sir Hugh. How may I serve you?"

"Has Gaston Miller recently purchased nails from you?"

"Aye. Mill wheel needed repair."

"How many nails did you make for him?"

"Hmm. Seven, I believe."

I thanked Janyn for his reply and hurried back to the mill. I could not remember how many nails I had seen fixing the new plank in place.

Gaston was yet warming himself at his hearthstone, so did not see me stop to count the nails in his repaired wheel. There were six. What did this mean? Mayhap nothing. The seventh might be driven into a beam within the mill, where Gaston could hang empty sacks. Or it might have been used to slay Kendrick Wroe. From the appearance of the nails used to repair the wheel, a seventh of the same size would have been long enough to do the deed.

There was but one way to learn the length of the nails Janyn had made for Gaston. I must ask him.

So I did. From the mill I walked back to the smithy and banged upon Janyn's door once more. When he opened it, curiosity writ large upon his face to see me again this day, I asked about the nails he had made for the miller.

"Wanted nails of good size, 'e did," Janyn said. "The mill wheel gets rough use, 'e said, so 'e wanted nails what wouldn't snap, an' would penetrate deep enough so 'e could bend over the point so's to clinch the planks what was 'eld together."

"So how long were these nails?"

"'Bout twice the length of me middle finger," Janyn said, "an' near as thick through as me little finger."

"Nails that size should serve Gaston well," I said.

"Indeed."

A nail that long would also have pierced to a lad's heart if jabbed under his arm. Such a nail would have reached even a full-grown man's heart if shoved forcefully into the side of his chest.

"One more thing," I said. "Have you heard any rumors that a young woman has been spotted down by the brook in the early hours of the morning?"

"None at all," he replied, looking quite perplexed. "What business would a lass 'ave wandering about at dawn?"

I had no answer to that question. I felt sure that Gaston was trying to confound my investigation. But why?

I returned home to a simple supper of hanoney. The days grew longer, but not so long as to permit the sun to warm the town and realm. When darkness settled upon Galen House I barred the doors, and I and my spouse and children sought our beds. 'Twould be the last night of peaceful repose I would enjoy for many days.

Chapter 4

As the sun illuminated the tower of St. Beornwald's Church on Tuesday morning, Kate gave Bessie three pence and sent her to John Baker to purchase fresh loaves. An hour later she had not returned.

Kate was exasperated, assuming our daughter had met a friend, sent by her mother on a similar mission, and was gossiping whilst the fresh loaves cooled. Kate sent me to fetch Bessie, a chore which caused me to be nearly as perturbed with the lass as was Kate.

John Baker's home and oven are on the High Street. I saw smoke rising from his chimney as I approached. His was an occupation nearly as pleasant on a cold day as was Janyn's. What I did not see was Bessie, either alone or with a friend.

Even on a cool morning the baker's door was open, and I entered the bakery to find John withdrawing half a dozen loaves fresh from his oven. I thought for a moment Bessie might have been waiting for these new loaves, but a quick glance around the place told me she was not there.

John turned from his oven, slid the loaves onto a table to cool, then tugged a forelock and asked how he might serve me, it being unexpected that a man should come to him seeking loaves. This was women's work. He assumed I sought something else, as indeed I did.

"Has my Bessie been here to purchase loaves?" I asked.

"Nay," he answered.

This reply alarmed me. Bessie had always been a dutiful, obedient lass. I could not believe she would so abandon her normal self as to neglect the task Kate had assigned her. But she is at an age when children develop independent attitudes not always pleasing to their parents.

I departed the bakery and set off for Galen House. I was somewhat irritated, and as I walked I rehearsed the reproof Bessie would receive when I found her.

Kate's eyes widened when I entered Galen House alone and told her that Bessie had not visited the baker.

"What other lasses are her friends?" I asked. "Likely she is visiting one of them and has lost track of time."

"Rohese Louches and Joanna Wace are friends of hers, but she'd not be with either." Kate's brow wrinkled, and a tear drained from her eye. "Bessie is an obedient child. Sent to the baker, that's where she would go. Unless she could not."

"Why could she not?" I said.

"She was taking three pence to the baker."

"You think she was waylaid and robbed? What man would do something so witless as to steal from his bailiff's daughter? And if such a thing happened, why has she not returned to tell us of the theft?"

"Mayhap," Kate sobbed, "she cannot. Mayhap someone laid a cudgel across her head, and she lies senseless in some path between here and the High Street."

This was an abhorrent thought, but it seemed possible. "I will search between here and the bakery," I said.

"I should never have sent her out alone so early," Kate wailed, "when shadows are yet long, and scoundrels can hide in them."

I hurried from Galen House and retraced my steps to the High Street. I searched under every bush, looked into every toft, peered into a hen house belonging to Andrew Tuchet, and investigated every hint of a path leading from Church View Street and the High Street. Whilst searching, I met several folk who knew me and my family well. None had seen Bessie, and neither did I. Whilst I searched, I called her name. There was no reply.

Kate and John looked hopefully to me when I re-entered Galen House. When they saw that I was alone, their expressions clouded. Kate had told John of his sister's disappearance, and he seemed as ready to shed tears as his mother.

Kate had occupied herself with preparing dinner, although I could see that her heart was not in it. There must be a meal awaiting Bessie when she came home – so Kate told me later.

One searcher had not been able to find Bessie, but mayhap a dozen or so might. I hurried to Bampton Castle, found John Chamberlain, and told him 'twas urgent that I speak to Lord Gilbert.

A few moments later I was ushered into the solar. Lord Gilbert motioned to a bench, inviting me to sit, but I could not. Lady Joan studied me with her usual frown, and Lord Gilbert asked my business. I had hurried from Galen House to the castle and was short of breath. Between gasps, I told him of Bessie's disappearance and requested the aid of castle grooms and valets in finding her. Before I was halfway through the tale Lord Gilbert stood, his face flushed red with anger.

Even Lady Joan's countenance became creased with concern.

"No man will deal so with my bailiff's daughter," Lord Gilbert growled. "If she has not returned home, 'tis because she cannot. She has been harmed or taken."

His summation of the matter did not calm me.

Lord Gilbert strode to the solar door, threw it open, and called loudly for his chamberlain. John must have been nearby, for he was present in an instant.

"Seek Sir Jaket and Thomas. Tell them I need them now. This minute. Then go to the marshalsea and tell Sir William to come to the solar with his grooms. Valets will be erecting tables in the hall for dinner. Tell them to stop and report here. Immediately."

John hurried away and completed his tasks in little more time than it has taken me to write of it. Lord Gilbert and I fidgeted impatiently whilst the men who had been called to assemble did so. There were soon seventeen men gathered in the castle yard at the foot of the stairs to the solar. Lady Joan looked down on the assembly, and I saw that her usual sour expression had transformed to worry.

Most of those gathered in the castle yard had only a rudimentary knowledge of the reason for their presence. Others who knew more explained to them. The yard was a babble of agitated conversations until Lord Gilbert bellowed a command for silence. He was instantly obeyed.

He then turned to me and said, "Sir Hugh will explain what you are to do, and why."

I did, wasting no time on particulars, as 'twas my view that the sooner the search for Bessie began, the sooner she might be found. As I spoke, my eye fell upon Charles de Burgh, Lord Gilbert's nephew and page, who had been sent by his mother to learn the arts of chivalry from his uncle. The lad was woebegone. I thought I knew why. If his youthful ardor might advance the search for Bessie, I was pleased to approve it.

Lord Gilbert, as with other men of his station, is accustomed to giving orders. He did so once I had completed the recitation of Bessie's disappearance.

"Sir Jaket, take Thomas and six others, and search Church View Street, Laundels Lane, and the church. If the vicars ask what you are about, tell them, and invite them to aid the search. Sir Hugh, take six others and search the High Street, Bushy Row, and the lane to St. Andrew's Chapel. Those remaining, come with me. We will search the Weald and the forest toward Cowley's Corner. Gather here if you find the lass, or when it comes dark."

Evening settled upon the town with no clue as to where Bessie might be. As part of my search, I sought the friends my wife had mentioned, Rohese and Joanna. Although word of Bessie's disappearance had spread through the town, they were as ignorant of where she might be as was I.

That evening I could not consume the pomme dorryse Kate had prepared. Neither could she. Even John, whose appetite is never wanting, left a sizeable portion on his trencher.

Sleep deserted me that night. A waning moon eventually gave dim light to our bedroom. I sensed that Kate, although inert, was as sleepless as I. The only sound in the chamber was of Gilbert's gentle breathing. The infant had only just begun to sleep through the night, much to Kate's delight.

I stared at the ceiling and reviewed what I and others had done so far, the places we had searched, and I tried to think of places which should have been examined but had not been. It occurred to me then that throughout the search for Bessie I had not once thought of the slaying of Kendrick Wroe. I sat bolt upright in bed. Was this the reason Bessie had been taken? Did some man wish me to seek my daughter rather than him?

My upright position startled Kate. "Wha . . . what has happened?" she said.

"Nothing. A troubling thought has come to me. Mayhap our Bessie has been taken to distract me from the search for whoever pierced Kendrick Wroe."

"This would be a man who has already done murder," Kate said.

"Aye. A man cannot hang twice even if he has slain two."

"But if he harmed our Bessie, he would no longer have her safety to hold over you."

"We must hope he considers that. But a man desperate enough to take Bessie is not thinking straight."

It would be inaccurate to write that I awoke early on Wednesday morning. A man who has not slept does not awaken. As dawn began to lighten the windows of Galen House I crept from our bed. Kate had finally fallen into a troubled sleep, and I did not wish to wake her.

I failed. Kate sat up in bed and looked at the glowing window. As she did so, Gilbert shifted in his crib. His breakfast was no work of mine, so I drew on chauces and cotehardie, then descended to the kitchen.

A few coals from Tuesday's fire yet glowed upon the hearth. I blew on them to produce a flame and promptly became light-headed. 'Tis a wonder I did not topple face first into the ashes.

Several carefully placed sticks were soon blazing, and moments later Kate entered and held her hands out to the warmth. 'Twas a fast day, which was just as well, as neither Kate nor I could summon an appetite. We shared a maslin loaf, which felt like feathers in my mouth.

"Who might have slain Kendrick?" Kate said. "In the night you said the villain might have seized Bessie to distract you from pursuing him."

"I cannot point an accusing finger at anyone. Maurice Motherby found Kendrick dead, half in, half out of Shill Brook. Thomas Rous did not seem surprised that Kendrick had perished in the stream. He is a sturdy lad. Could he have had aught to do with Kendrick's death? Mayhap Kendrick, in an unguarded moment, spoke to William Lacy of his success in taking fish from Shill Brook. Would the lad have shared this information with his father? And then there is Gaston Miller, who purchased large nails from Janyn," I concluded. "One of which could make a wound like a slender dagger. And he seems to know more about the murder than he is letting on."

"So Maurice, Thomas, William, Philip, and Gaston may have reason to divert you from a felony," Kate replied. "Might there be others you know not of?"

"Probably," I said. "But a more thorough search of the homes of these five seems a good place to begin today."

"Would a man who seized Bessie keep her nearby?" Kate wondered.

"To do so might leave him open to discovery. But he would likely keep her in bondage, so would want to be close enough to examine the ropes and knots to see that they held. And Bessie would need to be fed."

"Are you sure of that?"

"Nay. But our daughter dead would be of no use to a man who wished to hold her life over me."

"Only if you did not know that she had perished." Kate choked on the words.

I wondered if, after Tuesday's failed search, Lord Gilbert, Sir Jaket, and the grooms and valets would be amenable to renewing the quest. I need not have worried. Most of Tuesday's searchers were already assembled in the castle yard, the castle being their residence. Lord Gilbert was among them.

Janyn Wagge joined the party, giving up the profit a day's labor might bring. None of the men and boys I thought might know something of the death of Kendrick Wroe were present. If Janyn had heard of the hunt for Bessie, would not these others also have heard? Did their absence signify anything?

I told Lord Gilbert of the thoughts which had kept me awake in the night. He assigned the searchers to the four houses in which three men and two lads resided. Lord Gilbert sent me, Janyn, and two grooms to the mill. All were instructed to report back to the castle at noon, when, if Bessie had not been found, a fast-day meal would be provided.

The morning's effort was not successful. Janyn, the grooms, and I scoured the mill, seeking especially hidden places where the dust might have been disturbed. I pried up a floorboard where I thought two planks seemed suspiciously clean. Gaston protested this vigorously.

"What would I want with the girl?" he barked.

My cheeks flushed in response to his flippant attitude toward the abduction of my dear Bessie. I determined not to rise to the bait and focused instead on getting to the bottom of the situation. I knew that Kate and John – not to mention Bessie – were relying on me to maintain my composure and find our beloved girl.

I asked Gaston about the extra nail he had purchased from Janyn. He showed me where he had driven it into a beam, and the sack suspended from it. Janyn identified the nail as his work.

Lord Gilbert took grooms and valets with him to the Weald to inspect Philip Lacy's hovel. Lord Gilbert had no authority there, the Weald being the bishop's fief, but who would say nay to a great baron of the realm if he desired access to their house? There were few hidden places in such a simple dwelling. By all accounts the search was thorough, but swift and unproductive.

Philip's wife kept a few hens in a ramshackle structure behind the toft. The peevish hens were evicted whilst a groom was assigned to inspect the place. I suspect he was no more pleased with his task than the hens.

Sir Jaket led a party of valets to search Maurice Motherby's house. Motherby clearly resented this, Sir Jaket said. So much so that the knight thought he might be close to finding Bessie. Why else would the man be so incensed? Yet Bessie was not found.

Thomas, Sir Jaket's squire, took three grooms to search the home of Thomas Rous's parents on Bushy Row. They knew of Bessie's disappearance, Thomas's father Aymer said, and whilst protesting that neither they nor their son knew anything of her disappearance, they were cooperative to prove it so.

Dinner at the castle, I am told, was a solemn affair. When the search parties reported no success, I departed the castle for Galen House to inform Kate of the failure.

"Is she gone for ever?" Kate sobbed.

"Not if I, or Lord Gilbert, or Sir Jaket, or Janyn Wagge, or a dozen valets and grooms can prove otherwise," I said.

"Will the search continue this afternoon?"

"It must," I said. "I will return to the castle and discuss with Lord Gilbert what options remain open to us."

Kate had prepared a simple pea and bean pottage flavored with onions. I had gone without a decent meal for so long that I finally found appetite to consume an ample portion. Then 'twas back to the castle.

"If the lass is not held in some house," I said to Lord Gilbert, "which she may yet be, and the villain's residence not yet identified, it may be that she is secured in some wooded place."

"In which case," he replied, "she must be found before the cold takes her. She'd not be bound in a meadow or new-plowed strip, so I'll send the searchers into forest places this afternoon."

Search parties were assigned to wooded areas from Cowley's Corner in the west to St. Andrew's Chapel in the east. 'Twas nearly dark when we all assembled again at the castle. Lord Gilbert had advised that we call out Bessie's name as we probed the forests about Bampton, and I was hoarse from the shouting.

Chapter 5

Clouds had gathered during the day, and a cold, misty rain began to fall. Lord Gilbert did not speak of this new danger. He did not need to. To be cold is peril enough. Could Bessie survive being cold and wet both? My prayer, as I returned to Galen House, was that she was restrained in some house which was yet undiscovered.

I slept fitfully that night, exhausted as I was. My mind churned over the events of the past days, but eventually Morpheus overcame my despair. So 'twas Kate who heard the rapping upon the door of Galen House. She elbowed me in the ribs and told me to listen.

I did, and I heard a soft tapping. Then a barely audible voice whispered, "Father, 'tis me, Bessie."

I leapt from my bed, not bothering to draw on chauces and cotehardie, and hurried in the dark to the stairs, where I nearly tumbled in my haste.

I threw up the bar, pushed open the door, and, in the dim light of a waning moon, saw my disheveled daughter. Disheveled, wet, and shivering with cold, but alive.

"Is it Bessie?" Kate called from the top of the stairs.

"It is," I shouted.

I grasped my trembling daughter and led her to the kitchen hearth, where a few embers produced some small warmth. I placed wood upon the glowing coals and blew – carefully – to tease the flames from the embers.

Kate appeared with dry kirtle, braes, and cotehardie, and expelled me from the kitchen whilst she helped Bessie out of her soaked clothing and assisted her into dry garb.

Once this transformation into dry attire was accomplished, I drew a bench close to the growing fire. Bessie sat on it and, with shaking voice, answered my questions. She had, she said, been near to the baker's oven on her errand when a sack was thrown over her head.

"By one man, or more?" I asked.

"One," she said. "At least, were there two or more, they did not speak.

"I was thrown to the ground," she continued. "The man placed a knee in my back and pulled my hands behind, where he tied them tight. He held a hand over my mouth at first, but when I cried out he swatted me over my head and threatened harm unless I was silent. I should have disobeyed.

"Once my hands were tied tight he bound my ankles, then wadded a cloth into my mouth. I tried to spit it out, but with the sack over my head and hands tied behind my back I could not.

"I lay on the cold ground all day, but not alone. I could hear my captor moving, breathing. Through the sack I could see night coming. Before that I heard you call my name but dared not answer. The wool in my mouth would stifle any cry, and the man had threatened to strike me if I tried.

"When 'twas full dark, the man tossed me over his shoulder and carried me off. I knew you would search for me, but would not know where to look.

"The man left me for a time, I think. I heard nothing for what must have been several hours, then footsteps came close and I hoped I was found. Not so. The man produced more rope and tied me to a tree.

"From behind the tree, where I could not see him, he lifted the sack, then tied a blindfold about my eyes. I soon learned why. He gave me half a maslin loaf and something to drink. All this time I tried to remember whose voice it was I heard. I could not. He spoke few words, and these in a growl, like some wicked beast.

"Once I had eaten the loaf, the sack went over my head again and the rag was shoved back into my mouth. The man then untied my ankles and loosed me from the tree, and told me I could walk a few paces to deal with needs. He brushed a club aside my leg and told me if I tried to run he would lay the cudgel aside my head. When I had dealt with my necessities, he again bound my ankles and tied me to the tree."

"Did you hear men calling your name yesterday?" I said.

"Aye. I tried to reply, but the wool stifled my cries. My captor was away. He did not threaten me to be silent, so I think he must have been absent. Those who called for me did not come close enough that they heard my smothered cries.

"Even with the blindfold again in place I could tell when darkness fell. And then it began to rain. I was so cold and afraid, Father. I tugged on the cords about my wrists and discovered that the wet had caused them to stretch. I hesitated to try to pull free, for fear that my captor was close by. But he was not."

"He sought a roof over his head," I said, "leaving you out in the rain."

"Aye. The hempen rope slackened enough that I was able to draw my hands free. Then it was a simple matter to discard the sack and blindfold, spit out the gag, untie my ankles, and set off for home.

"At first I did not know where I was, but shortly I came to Shill Brook beyond the Weald. From there the way home was plain. I kept to the shadows and dark places in case my captor discovered I had fled and sought me."

"This is why you tapped so lightly upon the door," Kate said, "and whispered your name?"

"Aye."

'Twas well that Bessie had been able to free herself from the wet rope. Once it dried it would have been stiff, resulting in her being trussed even tighter.

I did not need to ask Bessie if she was hungry. Kate produced maslin loaves and cheese, and we broke our fast. John had awakened, wondered at the sound of voices in the night, and joined us as Bessie completed her tale. He was wide-eyed in response to his sister's harrowing experience.

I have enjoyed many tasty meals in my life, but none so satisfying as these loaves.

Lord Gilbert and the other searchers needed to be told of Bessie's escape. Then, with Bessie's guidance, some of us would seek the tree to which she was tied. Perhaps there might be a clue as to the identity of the felon who had seized my daughter.

But not yet. Bessie was warm after being chilled and had food in her stomach. Her head drooped and I told Kate to put her to bed. Whilst Bessie slept, I would go to the castle and tell Lord Gilbert and the others that Bessie had been found. Or rather that she had found herself.

I told Kate that under no circumstances must Bessie be permitted to leave Galen House alone. Her thwarted abductor might try to take her again if he saw the opportunity.

A dozen or so men had gathered at the foot of the stairs to the solar, awaiting Lord Gilbert and me, and directions for a new search. There was much joy when I told them Bessie was home, and much regard for her contriving a way to free herself. I noticed Charles de Burgh looked particularly pleased and relieved to hear my news.

Lord Gilbert heard the men's expressions of pleasure and satisfaction from the solar, appeared at the door, and soon learned the cause of the elation.

"Bessie," I said, "is exhausted and sleeping. When she awakens, I want her to lead me to the wooded place where her abductor held her."

"I will accompany you," Lord Gilbert said. "Shall we say after dinner?"

Several others volunteered, including Sir Jaket and Thomas. I was gratified at this support, and told them I would return with Bessie at the sixth hour.

Bessie slept 'til dinner, and likely would have continued so 'til supper had I not awakened her. I feared her abductor would find that she was away from where he had left her and, dreading identification, remove all trace of his presence.

Kate had prepared fraunt hemelle for our dinner. Bessie, usually loquacious at meals, was yet hungry after her ordeal, so concentrated on assuaging her appetite. She had told us already what happened to her. There was little more to say.

I told her, as I had told Kate earlier, that she must not leave Galen House except in the company of me or her mother. "When you finish your dinner," I said, "we will go to the castle. Lord Gilbert and I, and several others, will follow your lead to the place where you were tied. Mayhap your captor has not yet returned to the site, and we may find remains of the rope and blindfold and sack which you left behind. Or, if he has returned, mayhap in haste to be away from the place, he may have overlooked some item which could lead us to him."

Several of those who had spent two days seeking Bessie were awaiting us in the castle yard. Bessie's return, they thought, was but half their obligation. They wished to see him who had carried her off taken and have him brought to account for his felony, and the best way to do this was to find the last known place where he had been.

The cold rain had stopped, but the grass was wet and the ground muddy. Lord Gilbert and Sir Jaket were shod with oiled boots, so their feet were dry. We others had cold, wet feet by the time we left the banks of Shill Brook and entered the wood where Bessie had been kept.

She was uncertain of the exact location, as she had fled the place in the night and had seen nothing she could remember to assist in finding the tree to which she had been tied.

'Twas Sir Jaket who discovered the flattened leaves and snapped twigs which showed where Bessie had been held. The soggy oak leaves were especially crushed at the base of the tree to which Bessie had been bound.

But there was no discarded rope, no blindfold, no sack. The villain had returned, seen that Bessie was gone, and apparently carried away all objects which might have led us to him.

Had he guessed that Bessie had freed herself, or did he believe that the searchers - and he surely knew of the quest - had found her? I suggested to Lord Gilbert that the area around the tree where Bessie had been tied be examined for a distance of four or five paces. Mayhap the villain was in such haste to flee with rope, blindfold, and sack that he might have overlooked some thing which might prove evidence against him.

Charles, Lord Gilbert's nephew and page, with the keen eyes of youth, saw the dagger under a scraped-up pile of leaves. The blade was thin, no wider than my smallest finger, but long. 'Twas the type of dagger which, if ill-used, would easily snap unless made of the finest steel, and it did not appear to be.

Bessie's captor had likely found her gone, collected rope and sack and gag and blindfold, and departed the place in such haste that he had lost his dagger. And either did not know of the loss or had been fearful to return when he discovered it.

This discovery seemed to vindicate Gaston. Why use a nail to slay Kendrick if you possessed a dagger? Or was the dagger also his?

Charles held the blade before him and voiced a whoop of glee. Then he turned to Bessie and, with a grin, displayed it for her inspection.

Lord Gilbert, considering himself a man of martial acumen, took the dagger from the lad and held it before himself for a close examination. "Not of finest quality," he said, "but too costly for a cotter."

This assertion would eliminate Philip Lacy and his lad. They probably thought themselves fortunate if they owned a knife sharp enough to cut a fletch of bacon. And even for this they would have had little need, as flesh was likely foreign to their cooking pot.

Could Thomas Rous be a suspect? He had told Bessie he did not believe Kendrick had died of cold in the brook, but of some other cause. If not the cold, then to what would Thomas ascribe Kendrick's death? Had Kendrick been meeting with a young lass down at the brook? One whom Thomas had set his sights on, perhaps? Might this have led to an argument between the friends, a struggle, and the subsequent death of the lad? I still struggled to believe that any lady should have been wandering about at that hour. And surely Thomas would not have pointed to murder if he were the killer. Would he?

Mayhap Gaston did possess a dagger, and had used it against Kendrick. The fact that he had purchased more nails than he required did not mean he had used one against Kendrick before driving it into a beam. Bessie's abductor must have been a sturdy fellow to throw her over his shoulder, and Gaston certainly met that description, but why should he want to kill one child and abduct another?

Come to think of it, Philip Lacy might have possessed a stolen dagger. Or found one. If so, would he not have sold the weapon so as to provide something more useful for his family? Mayhap a poor cotter would consider a dagger, even one of poor quality, a possession to be valued. How could I enter a man's mind to know his thoughts?

If Philip Lacy did own a dagger, might William have known where it was kept and used it against Kendrick? If the two lads had come to blows over some disagreement, or over a young lady, William would likely have been the loser, being so slight. A dagger would have evened the contest. But William was too undersized to toss Bessie over a shoulder and carry her off.

Chapter 6

When Thomas Rous was found dead the next day, there was no doubt as to the cause. His corpse was not found anywhere near Shill Brook, but in a lane off the High Street. Several wounds to the poor lad's belly had bled copiously. Will Shillside was called, and his coroner's jury took one look at the bloody wounds and pronounced that murder had been done.

This ended Will's responsibility and began my own.

As with Kendrick Wroe, Will had rapped upon the door of Galen House shortly after dawn to tell me of the death. I knew someone had died in the night, for the passing bell rang from the tower of St. Beornwald's Church as I lay drowsing in my bed. But this time the cause was not in doubt. The lad's corpse lay where it was found, awaiting my examination.

Two children murdered in a matter of days. I found this news difficult to swallow. Had Thomas been slain in the night? His corpse had been found at dawn. When I turned the body, I observed that rigor mortis had not yet stiffened the corpse. I wondered, as I had with Kendrick, where Thomas had been going so early in the day.

I learned that where the lad's corpse was found and where he had been pierced were two different places. A blood-speckled trail led from an alley toward the High Street, as if Thomas, after he was stabbed, had tried to reach the street but failed, and collapsed where he was later found.

How much later? His parents knew not. Aymer and Anketil had been told of their son's murder and stood morosely as I followed the blood trail. Anketil wailed loudly. Aymer gazed upon his young son, stone-faced, but I saw a tear glisten in the corner of his eye.

The lad, he said to me, had been hired to goad the oxen of a plow team. He was not yet sufficiently brawny for the plow.

"Who hired your lad?" I asked.

"Maurice Motherby. 'Is mate is took ill."

Here was arresting information. Maurice had found Kendrick Wroe, and it now turned out that Thomas Rous was on the streets at dawn because Maurice had employed him. But why kill the lad if he needed him in the fields?

One thing was sure. The dagger found amongst the leaves where Bessie was held had not slain the Rous lad. It might, however, have pierced Kendrick. How many daggers might be found in Bampton?

I now had the slaying of two youths to solve. I had made little progress in untangling Kendrick's death. Now Thomas Rous had been added to my responsibilities. Were the two murders connected, or simply coincidence? Bailiffs do not believe in coincidence.

I thought I had established the reason Kendrick was slain, and had considered Thomas Rous a suspect in the death. That Thomas was now slain did not mean that he had not murdered Kendrick. Was Thomas slain in revenge? Had someone known more than I about Kendrick's death, and decided to slay the lad they suspected of the felony? Watkin Wroe did not seem to me a man who would kill another, but a man whose son is slain might do unpredictable deeds.

What kind of man would I become if a son of mine were slain, and the felon seemed likely to escape punishment? The thought troubled me, and I resolved to think on it no longer. Which is impossible. The more a man determines to drive a thought from his mind the more firmly embedded it becomes.

I had not broken my fast, so after releasing the corpse to Aymer and Anketil I hurried home for an early dinner. This was a simple meal, as 'twas a fast day. Bessie was bustling about the kitchen, pausing occasionally to stir a pot of peas and beans pottage while Kate sliced one of last year's onions into the pot for flavor.

Kate had heard Will announce the Rous lad's death, and told Bessie and John why I had departed Galen House without even a cup of ale or part of a loaf to sustain me.

After the meal, 'twas my obligation to call upon Lord Gilbert and inform him that there had been another murder in his manor. Was any other great baron of the realm so afflicted? Was any other bailiff so confounded? Probably. I do not know many other bailiffs, and those I do know are not apt to share their frustrations with another. Neither would I. 'Tis Kate who hears when some matter baffles me. As it did now.

I was reluctant to call upon my employer for two reasons. I did not want to present him with bad news, nor did I relish the scowl and pursed lips with which Lady Joan would surely greet me.

Since the outbreak of plague, and its return again and again, lords have difficulty finding tenants to work their lands. And pay rents. The Statute of Laborers requires that no lord can reduce his rents to entice tenants from some other manor to remove himself from another manor to his own. Nor can a tenant remove himself from one manor to another seeking a lower rent. And laborers must work for wages common in 1347, the year before plague appeared. This proscription is largely ignored. So the death of Thomas Rous may, at some future time, cost Lord Gilbert a few shillings each year. The dead do not rise from the churchyard to pay rents and fines.

As I passed under the portcullis, another concern wormed its way into my mind. I am employed, in part, to keep order in Bampton Manor. Two murders within a week cannot be considered orderly. Of course, if disorder when it occurs is not fatal, my surgical skills may remedy what chaos has produced.

If Lord Gilbert should decide to end my service to him as bailiff because of the turmoil in the town, I would have to leave Bampton. The practice of surgery in a small manor could not support Galen House and its inhabitants. I would have to move to Oxford and take up residence in Kate's dower house.

Physicians in Oxford are as thick as fleas on a hound, but few surgeons practice there, and most of those who do are barbers who augment their income by stitching wounds and setting an occasional broken arm. Such fellows do not have my training or skills, but would an injured man care? I would need to assure Lord Gilbert that I could and would get to the bottom of the two murders if I wished to maintain my role as bailiff. My family, and those of the two deceased boys, were dependent on my finding the wicked man who had carried out these atrocities.

I would also need to convince Lady Joan. I daresay the lady has influence and can direct Lord Gilbert's thinking. Few men can withstand a determined wife. All the more reason for a man to choose his wife wisely, as I have done. I must hope that Lord Gilbert has also, but I have my doubts. A wealthy widow needs neither beauty nor sagacity to attract an insolvent husband.

Lord Gilbert and Lady Joan were in the solar when I arrived, warm and with appetites contented with something more toothsome, I'm sure, than pea and bean pottage. Fish surely had been a part of at least one remove at the high table, and not stockfish, either. Valets and grooms would, like most folk in Bampton, be satisfied with a pea and bean pottage in some repulsive green hue. Much like my own meal.

My announcement did not surprise Lord Gilbert. News had come to the castle before tables were erected in the hall for dinner. And if castle residents knew of Thomas Rous's death, then 'twas certain all of Bampton knew of the felony.

"The lad had risen early to join a plow team, you say?"

"Aye. One of the team was ill. The odd thing is that the same man who found Kendrick Wroe dead – half in, half out of Shill Brook – was he who hired the Rous lad to work the oxen this day."

"Hmm." Lord Gilbert stroked his beard and lifted one eyebrow, as he is wont to do when perplexed. At one time I tried to emulate the trait, but soon gave up the effort. I wonder if his father, Richard, Second Baron Talbot, did the same. I suppose idiosyncrasies can, like wealth, be inherited.

"Remarkable," he continued, "that the same man is involved in both felonies. Should I have Sir Jaket pitch the fellow into the dungeon? A few days there might loosen his tongue."

Indeed it might. The builders of Bampton Castle had positioned the dungeon adjacent to the cesspit, and the placement of the stones, not all of them hewn true, allowed some of the filth to leak into the dungeon, with the accompanying stench. A man incarcerated there would be eager to find release. But would he speak the truth, or simply words he thought I and Lord Gilbert wanted to hear?

"Nay," I said. "If Motherby needed a lad to goad his oxen, why would he then slay the youth? It seems to me he would know, were he the felon, that I would put two and two together and link him to the deaths of Kendrick and Thomas. Unless he sees me as an uncomprehending dolt."

From the castle I walked to the Rous home. I found Anketil and two neighbors from the High Street washing the lad's corpse. This was no easy task. Thomas's wounds had bled copiously. The gore was dried and crusted, and his kirtle, braes, chauces, and cotehardie would have to be discarded, as stained and slashed as they were.

Aymer was sitting on a bench at his door as I approached. Would another examination of his lad's corpse tell me anything I did not already know? I could not be sure unless I did so. This I said to the bereaved father as he stood and tugged a forelock. He nodded, and showed me into the house, where I found the three women at their disagreeable task.

Aymer explained my presence to his wife, and she and her companions stepped back so that I might inspect the corpse unhindered. With clothing stripped away, I saw before me the body of a healthy youth. A lad who, provided he did nothing foolish, should have had many years of life before him.

First observations are not always thorough, so I began further inspection at the lad's head, where I parted his hair to see whether or not he had recently received a blow. He had not.

The arms were likewise free of bruises. No purple blemishes marred the youthful flesh. Thomas's torso was, of course, another matter. The two gaping wounds which had caused his death lay open and obvious. So obvious that they nearly distracted me from an anomaly. A healed scar on the lad's back.

I had asked the women to turn the corpse. For no good reason, as I now think on it. They did so, and the scar became visible.

Anketil saw me bend close to examine the scar and asked what I had found. I stood, pointed to the blemish, and asked when it had happened.

"Martinmas," she said, looking to her husband for confirmation.

"Aye," he said. "Day or so after."

"What happened?"

"'E was tusslin' with some other lads an' fell against a stick." Aymer rolled his eyes as he explained the wound. "Lads will be lads."

"Who were these friends?"

"Didn't say, did 'e."

I wondered if Kendrick or William Lacy had been among them. "You didn't come to me to have the puncture stitched closed," I said.

"Didn't see a need. Wasn't so great as to cause worry. If a man troubled you every time 'is lad suffered a cut or such you'd 'ave little time for your other duties."

This, I supposed, was probably true. I thought back to my own youthful incautious behavior. How did I survive such foolishness and grow to useful manhood?

Then again, if Aymer had thought to bring his lad to

me to have a puncture stitched closed, he would have considered the few pence I might charge for closing the wound and could have decided the injury would heal well enough on its own.

This explanation for the healed scar on the lad's back seemed satisfactory, so I instructed the women to turn the corpse to its back. His legs and feet were free of blemishes, but as I examined these a stray thought nagged at the back of my mind. It did not remain there, but pushed its way to the front.

"Turn the lad again," I said to the women.

They did so, but reluctantly. I could see in their expressions that they thought my examination bordered on disrespect of the dead.

Again, I studied the healed scar on the lad's back. A stick, it seemed to me, should make a round hole where it broke the skin, nature having made twigs and such mostly round, not flat. The healed blemish was not round. The edges were flat, the healed wound nearly as long as my forefinger – such as it would be if it were made by a long nail or a dagger. Did Aymer and Anketil suspect this? Had their son told them that tumbling to the ground upon a wayward branch had caused his hurt? Had they looked to see the cut? Or taken his word for it?

Mayhap the stick against which the lad said he fell had splintered. Would it then leave a flat-sided incision? Possibly. Perhaps I was making too much of an old injury when I should be concentrating my mind upon the wounds which slew the youth.

As it was Friday, the wake would be simple. A few loaves with no butter and, since the Rouses had the means, enough ale that the wake would become boisterous and loud. Indeed, Kate and I heard the vigil from Galen House before we set out to join it.

I covered the fire, Kate put John and Gilbert to bed, and I instructed Bessie that she must on no account raise the bars on the doors of Galen House, even if some man claimed to come from me with a message. Such an assertion, I told her, would be false. I would in no wise do so. We left a candle burning in the kitchen for light.

Was it important for Kate and me to attend the wake, even if briefly? Kate considered Anketil a friend, and I thought I might keep my ears open to the gossip of tongues loosened by much ale. Some man, or possibly men, knew what had caused the deaths of Kendrick Wroe and Thomas Rous, and might be persuaded by sufficient ale to reveal it.

Winter lingered. The night grew cold, and folk gradually stumbled home, their way dimly lit by the light of a waning sliver of moon.

I rapped upon the door of Galen House and called to Bessie. I heard her lift the bar in response to my voice and was, I admit, relieved that all was well. I soon learned it might not have been.

Bessie's face was pale in the dim glow of candle and fading moon. I sensed something was amiss and asked my daughter what troubled her.

"Some man," she said in a quavering voice, "tried the doors soon after you departed."

"Did he speak?" I asked.

"Nay, but I heard both doors rattle on their hinges, so I know he was present."

The night was calm. There was no wind to shake the doors. If the man did not speak, was it because he thought Bessie might recognize his voice?

I dropped the bars across the doors again, and Kate, Bessie, and I sought our beds. But I did not soon fall to sleep. Bessie was safe, but some man did not wish it so. I would remind her in the morning that she must not leave Galen House alone, although after her experience this night the admonishment would surely be unnecessary.

Maurice Motherby had moved to the top of my list of suspects. I decided to call on him after the lad's funeral.

Four men of Bampton carried the coffin, and, as with Kendrick, they were followed by a flock of keening women who did not cease their wailing until the coffin was set down under the lychgate. I watched the mourners carefully to see if any man behaved in an unseemly fashion. None did. Or if they did, I had not the wit to heed the anomaly.

Father Ralph spoke the homily at the funeral mass, then led us to the south side of St. Beornwald's Church, where he sprinkled holy water on the place chosen for Thomas's grave. The sexton and two assistants set to work with shovels and soon had a grave opened. But not too deep. Andrew was long-practiced at grave digging and knew, as with Kendrick's grave, that if he should excavate more than waist deep he would uncover some man's, or woman's, bones from a century or more past.

Thomas's corpse was lifted from the coffin and deposited gently into the grave. The coffin would be returned to Andrew Carpenter for future use. Mayhap this was the same box in which Kendrick Wroe had been carried to the churchyard. Likely so. Andrew would not go to the effort and expense of making two coffins if only one were required.

Maurice Motherby denied any complicity in the Rous lad's murder, as I knew he would, and invited me to call on his plow team mate who, as he had told others, was too ill to work.

The man in question, Peter Mainwaring, resided on Bushy Row. His wife answered my knock on her door and, when I asked of Peter, said, "He's no need of a surgeon."

The man crawled out from under a blanket, curious as to who was calling. His cheeks and nose were red, and he shivered violently. Motherby was correct. The man was ill, and my services could do little for him. I might offer a pouch of feverfew, but usually men afflicted like Peter recover with time, or they do not recover at all. They do not remain the same.

Peter sank back beneath his blanket as I bade him good day. Such a valediction is mere custom, but what else would I say? Commiserate with his discomfort, and suggest we might meet in the next world should he not recover his health?

One thing was certain: Maurice had not been lying about his ailing team mate, and his reasons for seeking out Thomas appeared to be genuine.

Winter had been long and hard. But by noon the sun had brought some warmth, and I thought daffodils might soon appear. Kate had prepared cyueles with Bessie's aid, so I was spared more green-complected pottage for my dinner.

It was our custom on warm summer evenings to draw a bench to the toft and chat whilst the setting sun warmed us and the west wall of Galen House. This day could in no way be construed as warm, and 'twas certainly not summer, but pleasant pastimes invite repetition. And my Kate, after listening to me express frustration about some matter, will often suggest some worthwhile course of action which had escaped my attention as we sit in the sun.

So after dinner I dragged a bench to the toft to enjoy the sun. There was little breeze to defeat the warming sun, so Kate joined me and we discussed the two slain lads and the possible felon - or felons - who had done the murders.

Bessie remained in the kitchen, at the domestic chores Kate had assigned her. Our conversation was suddenly interrupted by a scream, which was almost immediately stifled. Kate looked to me with alarm.

I knew instantly what had happened. Some man knew that Kate and I were not within Galen House. Perhaps he had heard our conversation whilst passing Galen House on Church View Street, peered around the corner of the house, seen us deep in conversation, and decided to attack Bessie.

I was on my feet immediately and scrambled for the kitchen door. I threw the door open and saw Bessie lying upon the flags, sobbing, and the back of a man fleeing out of the front door. I lifted my daughter from the floor, ascertained that she had suffered no hurt, and in so doing lost the opportunity to chase down the malefactor who had defiled my home. By the time I ran through the front door to the street, the man had disappeared.

The only way he could have done so was to turn down Rosemary Lane or duck into a house between Galen House and the lane. I knew and trusted all the folk who resided on Church View Street, so discarded the notion that the man who had violated Galen House occupied a dwelling between my home and Rosemary Lane.

I set off at a run toward Rosemary Lane, understanding as I did that the chase would likely prove futile.

It did. When I arrived at the lane I looked to the east, where it joined the High Street. 'Twas vacant. The man I sought was either fleet of foot, or had ducked into some toft and was even now creeping behind hen houses and shrubbery to make good his escape.

What would possess a man to enter Galen House and attempt to seize Bessie? Did he not know that she would cry out, even if briefly, before he could smother her scream? The fellow must have been desperate to take such a risk, or so foolish that he did not consider the hazard. Was he desperate enough to try such a thing again? If so, mayhap he was rash enough that, given another such opportunity, he might decide to silence Bessie with a dagger rather than a hand over her mouth. The thought made me shudder.

When Bessie was first taken, I had assumed 'twas an attempt to draw me away from seeking whoso had slain Kendrick. Now I began to wonder if there was another reason. Did Bessie know something about the murders? Perhaps something she knew but did not know that she knew. Did that make sense? It did, at least as much as any other thoughts which had come to me recently. Mayhap there was some truth to the rumor of a young woman wandering about at dawn. Might the lass have been one of Bessie's friends, Rohese Louches or Joanna Wace?

Kate was comforting our trembling daughter when I returned home, breathless after my fruitless pursuit. John, having heard Bessie scream, stood wide-eyed, old enough to know that there was much amiss in Galen House but too young to understand what. Bessie, sobbing, was likely questioning why she had been born the daughter of a bailiff.

Mayhap 'twould be no bad thing if Lord Gilbert decided my services no longer suited. Removing to Oxford and Kate's dower house would protect Bessie from the danger which now encompassed her in Bampton. But then, of course, in Oxford her blossoming beauty would attract lecherous young scholars, and I would be required to keep her safe within doors there as well. There are few safe places for a beautiful lass.

There came a thunderous knocking upon the door of Galen House whilst Kate and I calmed Bessie. Whoever pounded upon the door did so firmly enough to rattle the hinges. 'Twas Janyn. He likely thought he was striking the door gently.

"Saw you runnin' down Rosemary Lane," he said, "an' thought, when a bailiff runs through the town, it can mean no good thing. Banked me fire an' come to see did you need 'elp."

I explained to Janyn the reason for my sprint. As I did so, he looked past my shoulder and saw Bessie, red of eye, confirming my tale.

"The fellow got away, then," Janyn concluded. "No idea who 'twas?"

"None. It is difficult to identify a man from the rear. All backs appear the same."

"Aye," he agreed ruefully.

Actually, my assertion was not completely true. No man would have mistaken Janyn's broad back and shoulders for my slender physique.

"Well, if you've no need of my aid I'm off to the castle. Promised the marshalsea I'd 'elp with shoein' Lord Gilbert's dexter. A vicious beast, is Bucephalus. 'Specially he don't like 'avin' nails drove into 'is 'ooves. Takes two to do the job."

The horse, I thought, would have met his match when Janyn seized a leg.

Bessie was eventually calmed, and I assured her that, did her mother and I have tasks in some part of Galen House away from Church View Street, we would bar the front door so that no man might enter. How long could we live in such a fashion? And would we grow careless after a few days or weeks, and neglect to secure the door?

Whilst I thought on these matters, Janyn reappeared. "Lord Gilbert would have you bring Bessie to the castle," he said. "I told Sir William of the man who tried to seize your Bessie whilst me an' the farrier was shoein' Bucephalus. He told Lord Gilbert, an' Lord Gilbert sent me to tell you to send Bessie to him. John too, if you think whoso tried to take Bessie might threaten the lad if 'e can't get 'is 'ands on Bessie."

This appalling thought had not occurred to me. But now that Janyn had mentioned it, I knew the threat would not leave my mind until the felon who had slain Kendrick and Thomas was apprehended.

Kate had heard Janyn speak of Lord Gilbert's invitation. I could see in her eyes that the thought of John in peril was as new and unwelcome to her as it had been to me.

What of Gilbert? Was the babe also at risk? He was almost always either in Kate's arms or in his crib up the stairs. And what of Kate? If Bessie and John were out of the villain's reach, safe in the castle, would he turn to Kate for a hostage?

My entire family could not take up residence in the castle until I discovered a murderer, or murderers. Lady

Joan would never approve. I suspected she would not approve even of Bessie and John residing in the castle. She did not seem to approve much of anything. Having two children underfoot would certainly merit her disfavor. Yet if her distaste meant that Bessie and John would be safe from harm, 'twas a situation I could tolerate. Whether or not Lord Gilbert could, and for how long, was another matter.

Was all this distress related to my responsibility in finding out who had slain Kendrick and Thomas, or was there a more sinister but as yet hidden cause? It is difficult to solve a mystery when the mystery itself is a riddle.

The castle hall was prepared for supper when Kate and I arrived with Bessie and John. Kate would have remained at Galen House with Gilbert, the doors barred, but I had started to see miscreants wherever I turned, and I feared that even oaken doors and bars might not prevent some determined rogue from doing hamsoken.

When Lord Gilbert saw that I had entered his hall with my family, he ordered the high table expanded. My rank as Sir Hugh entitles me, Lady Katherine, and my children seats at the high table. I sensed that Lady Joan did not approve, but Charles de Burgh did. From the corner of my eye, I saw Lord Gilbert's nephew smile broadly, and not at me.

A fast day supper at Galen House might occasionally feature stockfish, or perhaps mussels. But there would not be three removes, as there were this day for the high table. Lord Gilbert's valets and grooms contented themselves with a pea and bean pottage, although their meal may have included a few fragments of stockfish.

As for us at the high table, we enjoyed eels in bruit for the first remove, a pottage of whelks for the second, and sops in fennel for the third. I began to fear that Bessie and John might so enjoy such a menu they would be disappointed once I had discovered the murderer and they must return to Galen House.

'Twas dusk, the hall dimly lit by candles and cressets, by the time the void, a pottage of pears and cherries, was served. Lord Gilbert saw my uneasy glances toward the darkening windows, and assigned Sir Jaket and his squire Thomas to accompany Kate and me to Galen House. We arrived there without incident. If any man with evil intent observed our progress, the passing shadows of a sword-bearing knight and a squire with a dagger dissuaded him of any foul intentions he might have had.

Chapter 7

I awoke at dawn to the peal of the passing bell. 'Twas too early for the sexton to call folk to mass. Along with the other folk of Bampton, I wondered who had perished in the night. I drew on chauces and cotehardie, and sought Father Thomas's vicarage. His clerk answered my knock.

"Peter Mainwaring," Gerard said, "died in the night."

I remembered Peter's ghastly appearance twenty-four hours earlier and was not much surprised at this report. There would be another wake this evening, and another funeral mass and burial tomorrow, and Maurice Motherby would need to find yet another man to join his plow team.

I returned to Galen House and banged upon the door so that Kate would admit me. We had together resolved that Kate would not remain alone with doors unbarred. As I was about to enter, I saw the dead man's son approach. Simon is a year or so older than John. Too young to wield an ox goad, although it is likely that his father and Maurice Motherby assigned him the task of treading on clods to break them smooth for better planting.

'Twas clear that Simon's intended destination was Galen House, so I waited at my open door for the lad to come near.

"I was sorry to learn of your father's death," I said. "I saw him yesterday and knew him to be quite ill."

"'Tis that me mother 'as sent me about," Simon said. "Took a turn for the worse last night. Fingers an' toes turned blue, like. Never seen plague do so, me mum said. Asked if you'd come see. Not like you can do aught for 'im, but she'd like to know what took 'im."

"I am a surgeon, not a physician."

"You'll not come?"

I admit to being curious about Mainwaring's death. I'd never seen or heard of a man fevered and red of nose and eyes suddenly dying with blue-tinged fingers and toes. Curiosity is said to have killed a cat or two. I did not think it would be fatal to me. I told the lad I would visit his mother after mass and my dinner.

'Twas not only Peter's fingernails and toenails which had a blue tint. His lips also had a blue hue. I have seen such coloration in folk in the past. Usually the old, who must sit and rest after taking only a few steps, their breath coming in gasps. In such folk it seems to me their heart is failing them. I once pressed an ear to the chest of a grizzled old fellow whose nails and lips were as blue as Peter's and listened for his heartbeat. It was faint and irregular. Not like the strong rhythm from the heart of a young man.

Was Peter so ill that his heart had failed him? That could be, I suppose. I am no physician, so cannot be certain. Although physicians who claim knowledge in such matters are certain of many uncertain things.

The vicars of St. Beornwald's Church would reap a handsome reward. Two lads and a man were dead in Bampton, their souls destined for the agonies of purgatory unless Father Thomas, Father Ralph, and Father Robert were paid to say prayers for their early release from that malign place. If such a place there be.

The monks of Eynsham Abbey presented me with a Bible for services I rendered the abbey a decade or so past. Nowhere in Holy Writ can I find purgatory mentioned. Would not such a consequential place be made known? Would the Lord Christ send a man to purgatory without first warning him to amend his ways for the better, to avoid many years assigned for punishment? I might be accused of listening to Master Wycliffe on this matter. And I'd be guilty.

I must write no more on this subject. The Bishop of Exeter has somehow learned of my views, and even sent a nephew to Bampton to serve the Church of St. Beornwald as vicar, but in reality it was to gather evidence against me. This conniving priest was recalled when Lord Gilbert learned of his lecherous behavior toward Kate's servant, Adela Parkin, and demanded his removal. His replacement, Father Robert Astley, is a great improvement. But even he will not refuse the coins of the poor to pray for early release from a non-existent place.

As I examined Peter Mainwaring's corpse, Maurice Motherby entered the house. "'Eard the passing bell," he said. "Wondered if it might be for Peter, him bein' so ill."

"You'll need to find another man to join you in a plow team now," I said.

"Aye."

Maurice appeared distressed by Mainwaring's death, but perhaps more so by the idea of having to find a new partner. Plague has so reduced the supply of laborers that 'tis difficult to replace one who has perished. Maurice would have to search far and wide to find a new colleague.

"Called in last night to see if Peter would be well enough today to return to plowin'," Maurice volunteered. "'E was yet ill, but didn't seem near to death."

"His illness did not take him," I said. "Some new malady struck him down. Mayhap this second affliction was caused by the first, but I've not known coughs and sneezes, and reddened eyes and noses, to produce blue lips and fingers and toes, and then death."

Maurice went outside when Peter's wife and a neighbor began to wash the corpse. Rigor mortis had not yet stiffened Peter, so they were able to turn him easily. Margaret sobbed occasionally as she worked, and between sobs she spoke, as if silence were a thing to be avoided.

"Maurice is a good man," she said. "Sat with Peter last evening 'til past dark."

"Peter was strong enough to converse with him?"

"Oh, aye. When I took to bed, Peter told me 'e thought 'e was better. Told Maurice 'e'd be able to work again in a few days." More sobs. "But when I awoke this mornin', Peter wasn't warm like 'e 'ad been, but cold an' blue. Dead, 'e was. Died in the night, whilst I slept beside 'im." Margaret shuddered. There followed another period of sobs. She was not alone in this. Behind me I heard the lad, Simon, and his two younger sisters also weeping softly.

Margaret would not be a widow for long, I suspected. I knew of four men of Bampton and the Weald whose wives had perished and would be keen to remarry. One woman had died in childbirth, one when plague returned, and another was scalded to death when she tripped on a hearthstone and fell against a kettle of boiling water. She died in great agony. There was nothing I could do for her. Another simply died. Folk sometimes perish for no reason known to physicians and surgeons.

I did know of an herb which could slay a man, and which might cause lips, fingernails, and toenails to take on a blue tint as he died. Monkshood is sometimes helpful to reduce pain, but I will not use it. Employed in too great an amount, it is a deadly poison. Crushed hemp seeds and dried lettuce sap dissolved in ale are preferrable. Not, perhaps, as potent to relieve pain, but far safer.

Where and when would Peter have consumed monkshood, if indeed he had done so? Was there another herb which, when consumed, might cause death in the same manner as Peter had died?

There are several. Hemlock, woad, foxglove, and deadly nightshade are killers when used over-generously. The Lord Christ has provided men with many medicinal herbs, but some must be used frugally, or their consumption can be worse than the disease or hurt they are administered to alleviate.

Another conversation with Maurice Motherby was in order. The last man to converse with Peter before his death, he had remained outside the Mainwaring home while I spoke to Margaret.

"Last evening, when you spoke to Peter, you had no thought that he might perish in the night?" I said.

"Nay. Seemed hale an' on the mend."

"But you also said that, when you heard the passing bell, you thought it might toll for Peter."

"Didn't know of any others ill in Bampton or the Weald."

"Peter died with blue-tinged lips and finger- and toenails. When you spoke to him last night, did you notice this?"

"His 'ands an' feet was under the blanket, wasn't they? But now you mention it, 'is lips was pasty, like."

"Have you given any thought to the man who will join you now in a plow team?" I said.

"Aye. I intend to ask Stephen Parkin."

Stephen is Adela Wagge's father, father-in-law to Janyn Wagge, and a poor cotter, barely able to keep the wolf from the door. 'Twas surely a relief to his thin purse when Adela found employment as Kate's maid, then wed Janyn so that she no longer ate at his meager table. Parkin would be pleased to serve Maurice and thereby earn a few pence. He was a tenant of the Bishop of Exeter, as he resided in the Weald, but the vicars of St. Beornwald's Church, the bishop's agents in the Weald, would not deny Parkin a chance to better his state by working for one of Lord Gilbert's tenants. Most of those who manage estates demand that their tenants labor only for the lord of the manor. Since plague has struck and returned time and again, workers are scarce and not to be shared.

Parkin was no stranger to murder; his wife Emmaline having been a suspect in the killing of Edmund Harkins some years earlier. Back then I had found the man evasive, to say the least, but then what man would not do all in his power to protect his wife from the King's Eyre, given half a chance? I had no reason to suspect Parkin of Kendrick's, Thomas's or Peter's deaths, nor of Bessie's abduction. He might be a man of meager means, but that does not a murderer make.

Priests frown on the disorderly mob which can result from too much ale consumed at a wake. Especially on a Sunday. Mayhap one of the vicars had words with Margaret, for there was no wake for Peter Mainwaring Sunday evening. Word filtered through the town that the wake would be Monday evening. How Margaret was persuaded to wait a day, I do not know. Perhaps the vicars threatened to assign Peter to a grave on the north side of the church.

Should Kate and I attend the wake? It would show respect to do so, and Gilbert could accompany us. No man would risk trying to take Kate or Gilbert with dozens of folk surrounding them, making merry with Margaret's ale. So I thought.

The evening was mild, which was welcome after so harsh a winter. Had the night been cold, the number of folk who left their hearths to honor Peter might have been smaller. In which case, the miscreant who appeared out of the gloom and threw Kate and Gilbert to the ground might have made a clean escape. He did escape, but 'twas not clean.

The rogue could have had no hope of abducting Kate. Not while I was present and able to shout for aid against him. Which I did.

We were no more than a hundred paces from the wake, returning to Galen House, and my cry for help brought a dozen men at a run. Some of these had consumed enough ale that their approach was uneven, but most headed straight toward me.

Meanwhile, I dove for the legs of the man who had thrown Kate to the ground. 'Twas too dark to identify the scoundrel. A sliver of waning moon would not rise 'til past midnight, and the candles and cressets providing some small illumination to the Mainwaring toft did not produce enough light to see anything but a shadow.

Gilbert had been asleep in Kate's arms. She had tried to protect him as she was knocked off her feet, but the babe was jolted awake when they hit the ground. He responded with a wail, as would any babe. Mayhap this disconcerted the assailant. He kicked to free himself from my grasp and succeeded. But not completely. A shoe remained in my hand as the knave ran off into the dark.

The men who had run from the wake stopped to discover the cause of my cry for help. In so doing they allowed the rogue to escape into the night, for by the time I explained what had happened he was well away.

Four men volunteered to walk with us to Galen House and see us home safely, for which I was grateful. What the assailant had hoped to accomplish by falling upon Kate I could not imagine. Even now, as I write of the event, knowing who was guilty, I am perplexed. But not all men think as I do, nor act from the same motives. The reader may decide if that is good or ill.

Once the doors of Galen House were barred and our home secure, I lit a cresset and examined the shoe I had snatched from the assailant's foot. A more complete examination must await daylight, but from the dim light of the cresset flame I could see that the shoe was far from new.

Kate began to weep whilst I examined the shoe. "Will we ever again be safe in Bampton?" she sobbed. "Has all this mayhem occurred because you seek whoso slew Kendrick Wroe?"

"Probably. I cannot guess what other act of mine should bring such wrath down upon us."

"At least Bessie and John are safe in the castle."

"They are. Now come, and we shall soon be safe abed."

Safe, but not asleep. Kate could not calm herself. Who could, after being so set upon? Nor could I. No man can rest easy after his wife has been attacked.

We both heard Kate's rooster announce the dawn after a restless night. The only good thing which can be said for this night was that we were warm under a blanket as we lay awake.

I re-examined the shoe in the light of day. It was not tattered with age and use, but 'twas not new. Many years past I had discovered a felon by his torn shoe heel, so I paid particular notice to this heel. Was there any telling pattern or mark the shoe would make on a muddy path? Nay, other than the fact that it was well worn. As were the shoes of most Bampton residents. Must I walk Bampton's streets with my head down, seeking the mark of a worn shoe in the mud? I could not take ten paces without seeing such an imprint. The shoe had, I could see, been worn on the man's right foot. That reduced the number of footprints I must track by half.

There is no cobbler in Bampton. Those who desire new shoes must travel to Witney or Oxford, where several men follow the trade. Since the assailant's shoe was now in my possession, mayhap I should ask them to keep eyes and ears open to learn if any man of Bampton or the Weald had limped off to Oxford to purchase a replacement shoe. I supposed 'twas possible that, old as this shoe was, Kate's attacker might own an even older pair, and put one or both of these back into use.

I had some knave's shoe. What good would my possession of it do? I flung it down in disgust.

Kate had watched me examine the shoe. She picked it up and turned it in her hands, as I had done. "What have you learned?" she asked.

"Not much," I replied. "'Tis an old, worn shoe, such as half the folk of Bampton and the Weald wear."

Kate finished her study of the shoe and was about to discard it when she stopped and reached a hand inside the shoe. I saw her lips purse in concentration.

"What have you found?" I said. I had been concentrating on the outside of the shoe, seeking some peculiarity which might identify the owner. Kate, with her smaller hand, had examined the inside of the shoe.

"I'm not sure," she said. "Something doesn't seem proper."

"Something?"

"I can only feel the imprint of four toes," she said. "There are dimples in the sole for four toes, but I cannot feel a fifth. Here," she offered.

I took the shoe from her, but try as I might I could not get my hand deep enough into the shoe to feel any depressions in the leather made by toes in a well-worn shoe.

I keep my scalpels in a chest in our bedroom. I stood up from the bench, told Kate what I intended, and returned shortly with a sharp blade. 'Twas a simple matter to slice through the leather and open the inner part of the shoe.

I saw clearly then what Kate had found. There was no indentation where the smallest toe of a man's right foot should have made an imprint. There were depressions for the other four toes, but not for the smallest.

"Do you know of a man who is missing a toe?" Kate asked.

"Aye. Harold Oakshott became careless with an adz some years past and lopped off two toes."

"Did you treat him?"

"Aye. But in such a case there is little a surgeon can do. I stitched closed what I could, then bound the wounds with linen strips to keep the filth from the lacerations. I gave him a pouch of crushed hemp seeds to mix with ale to reduce his pain, and suggested he be more careful in the future."

"Harold was surely pleased with the advice," Kate said.

"I suspect that this shoe belonged to some man who, in the past, was also incautious with some sharp tool. An ax, mayhap. And not recently."

"Not recently?"

"A man cannot shear off a toe without also removing a part of his shoe with it. This," I said, pointing to the gaping shoe, "has surely been worn by the same man for many years. He was not wearing it when he became careless with an ax."

"Will you seek a man who has lost his smallest toe?" Kate said.

"Aye, but I am unsure how to go about it. Mayhap I could ask Lord Gilbert to require that all the men of Bampton and the Weald show me their right foot."

"Would he do so?"

"If I explained why, he might."

Peter Mainwaring's funeral was on Tuesday morning. We heard the approaching mourners as we concluded our examination of the shoe. I could not imagine there would be any danger to Kate in daylight, but there has been much evil which no man imagined until he saw the result. So I told Kate to remain with Gilbert at Galen House, with doors barred, whilst I represented our family at the funeral.

The coffin, as with the rites of the past two weeks, was set down under the lychgate, thence carried to the church for the funeral mass, and from there to the churchyard. Father Ralph sprinkled holy water on the turf near to the east wall of the churchyard, and Andrew Pimm and his assistants went to work. Many more funerals, and the vicars of St. Beornwald's Church would need to see Andrew Carpenter about new spades. Those the sexton and his aides used were quite worn.

Once again, when the coffin was set down at the open grave, the lid was removed and Peter, wrapped in a shroud, was lifted from it to be lowered into the grave. The coffin would return to Andrew's shop, there to await another death.

As Peter was transferred to his grave, the linen shroud shifted and his feet were exposed. Pimm moved to cover them, so as to avoid humiliation to the corpse. Peter would not care, although Margaret might.

The sexton replaced the shroud quickly, but not before an anomaly caught my eye. I called to the sexton to stop his work. Then, with all eyes upon me, I told Pimm and his assistants to remove the corpse from the grave.

Folk gazed at me with wide eyes and open mouths as the corpse was drawn from the grave.

"Set Peter down here," I said, pointing to the turf alongside the grave. When this was done, I withdrew the shroud from Mainwaring's feet and ankles so as to study the red blemish which, moments earlier, had caught my attention.

A red stain about the size of my palm, and two small spots about as far apart as the width of a finger, were visible upon Peter's left ankle. If these had issued blood, the washing of the corpse had sluiced it away, but the punctures were yet visible.

Father Ralph saw me examining Peter's feet, peered over my shoulder, and spoke. "What is there? What have you found?"

I guessed immediately what I had seen – what it was which had turned Peter's lips and nails blue, and what had slain him. "An adder has bitten Peter," I said, and pointed to the red blemish and twin pricks the snake had made.

Margaret heard me and spoke. "When could this have

happened? He's not been at work in the fields for many days."

"He told you Saturday evening that he felt well enough that he would soon be able to return to his work, did he not?"

"Aye."

"But when you awoke on Sunday morning you found him cold, blue, and dead."

"Aye."

"Then he was bitten sometime in the night."

"But I was abed with 'im. Why did 'e not cry out?"

"I cannot say. Mayhap his sleep was so deep that the pricks of an adder's fangs did not awaken him."

"How would an adder get into our bed?"

"I do not know the way of snakes but that they seek warmth. What better place to find it on a cold night," I said, "than in a man's bed?"

"It might 'ave bitten me," Margaret said.

I stood, as did Father Ralph and Margaret. The sexton and his assistants resumed their task.

Among the mourners was Gaston Miller. I was surprised to see such a sorrowful face and heaving chest on a man who, as far as I knew, had little to do with Peter during his lifetime. Could the dramatic appearance of grief have been assumed for my benefit? But if so, why? No man could be responsible for the death of another by adder bite.

Peter was soon interred, and we who mourned began to disperse.

Because of my discovery, the funeral took longer than usual. Kate had begun to worry that something of an ill nature had happened to detain me. She had prepared let lardes for our dinner, and while we ate I told her of the marks on Peter Mainwaring's ankle.

"The snake did not also strike Margaret?"

"Evidently not."

"Mayhap an adder has only enough venom for one strike," Kate said. "Or mayhap it slithered into Peter's bed before Margaret joined him for the night."

"Both suggestions are plausible," I replied. "The only certainty is that Saturday evening he thought his illness nearly past and he could resume plowing Monday, and Sunday morning he was dead from an adder strike."

"Was the snake found?"

"Nay," I said. "No one thought to seek it. That Peter died of snake bite was not considered 'til an hour past, when I saw the red blemish and twin punctures on his ankle. By now the adder has probably moved away to some warm, hidden place."

"What would be warmer than a house?" Kate said. "The snake would not find a warm burrow in February."

"Nay," I agreed. "They do seek to spend the winter underground, I understand. Coiling a foot or so deep in the ground is apparently warmer than hunting for warmth above ground."

"I wonder," Kate said, "what would cause an adder to leave its burrow when the days have been so cold."

"The topic was never raised during my study of surgery at the University of Paris," I replied. "Until I discovered the snake bite, I thought poison might have been the cause of Peter's relapse and death, but I could not imagine who might have administered the fatal dose, or why."

"So now," Kate said, "you are relieved that his death was mischance and not murder."

"Aye, but that is what the coroner's jury first thought of Kendrick Wroe's death."

"And was wrong."

"Aye. You have reminded me that I have no killers in mind who might have slain Kendrick and Thomas. I do not even have evidence that the same man did both felonies. Mayhap the murders were done by two different men."

"You spoke of asking Lord Gilbert if he would require the men of Bampton to display their right feet, to see who might have a missing toe. If the man is found, and you press him, do you think he will confess to slaying Kendrick and Thomas?"

"And thereby place a noose about his neck? Not with the little proof I have. Can I send a man to the King's Eyre for assaulting my wife? Aye, I might. But as no lasting harm was done, the judges might release him with only a fine."

"Then you will not ask Lord Gilbert to request it of the men of his manor?" Kate said.

"I will ask."

Chapter 8

Lady Joan was with her husband in the solar when I did so. She heaped scorn upon the idea. This was no new thing. She seemed to scorn most of my suggestions.

"We already have this fellow's brats reading your book of hours. The lad I can understand. He will need Latin to take up studies at Oxford. But the lass . . . of what use is it to her to read Latin? Reading English is enough for any maid. It's more than most can do, no matter how high born. I myself read little, and the lack has done me no harm."

"Many men of Bampton and the Weald will lack a toe or two," Lord Gilbert said. "Such impairment is often the result of laboring with sharp instruments. Some may have been at Poitiers and lost toes to a French poleax. But they'd likely be too old by now to fall upon a lady in a dark street. I must agree with m'lady. You will need to find another way to discover your toeless knave. Now, as regards the lads recently found dead, what progress have you made in finding the felons who did the murders?"

"I am not sure," I replied, "that 'felons' is the proper term. There may be only one felon, and he is doing his best to interfere with my pursuit of him."

"Abducting Bessie being one of the ways he has tried to frustrate your effort?"

"Aye. And mayhap causing worry for my Kate's safety is another."

"You think the toeless assailant who knocked Lady Katherine down may be the same one who took Bessie?"

"Why else would a man do such a thing? Kate has made no enemies in Bampton."

"But you have," Lord Gilbert chuckled. "'Tis the way of things. Bailiffs have few friends. 'Tis why I pay you well . . . to do those disagreeable things I wish to avoid."

At the word "pay", Lady Joan's brow again furrowed to a scowl. This facial feature comes readily to her. I noticed that Lord Gilbert avoided her glare.

"Well," Lord Gilbert said, suddenly serious, "you must seek your knave without removing his shoe. Unless you can find a way of doing so which does not require my sanction."

Lady Joan seemed to approve. Her scowl faded and a look of triumph replaced it.

Next morning, Kate and I shared a maslin loaf and the last dregs of an ewer of stale ale. Responding to the empty ewer, Kate would normally have sought Milicent Baker to replenish our supply. But these were not normal days. I would not permit Kate to leave Galen House for any reason. I visited Milicent myself to fill the ewer, and whilst I was at this errand, I left Kate and Gilbert behind barred doors.

If Milicent was surprised that I was at Kate's usual chore, she hid it well. Mayhap she had heard of the attack against my wife.

I returned with the foaming ewer, then sat at the kitchen bench to plan my day. A part of my duty this day was to devise some way of discovering the felon who had slain Kendrick Wroe. If I could find a reason for a man to murder a lad whose only misdeed was poaching his lord's pike, I would go a long way to identifying the man. Kendrick's crime was against Lord Gilbert. Why should some other man care about the violation? This was a head-scratching question. I wondered if there could be any truth in Gaston Miller's insinuation that a young lass had been seen down at the brook. No lass of good reputation would have ventured out alone in the early hours, presumably to meet a young man in secret. Who else knew of the clandestine rendezvous, if such a thing had taken place? Or was the mention of a lady a mere fabrication on Gaston's part, designed to cast doubt away from himself?

I could not seek a felon whilst remaining in Galen House to protect Kate. But I was loathe to leave her in order to go about Lord Gilbert's business. I told her so.

"If you are not at Lord Gilbert's business," she said, "that harridan to whom he is wed will prod him to replace you. Then where will we be?"

"In Oxford," I replied. "Residing in your dower house, eking out a living amongst the physicians and barbers who inhabit the town."

"I would regret leaving Bampton," Kate sighed.

"As would I. So, though I dislike the thought of leaving you alone, I must be about the business of seeking a murderer."

As I approached Mill Street, I glanced to my left and saw Maurice Motherby and Stephen Parkin leading a brace of oxen toward St. Andrew's Chapel. They would turn aside before they came to the chapel and continue the plowing which Peter Mainwaring's illness had interrupted.

The plow had been left in the field, rather than hauling it from barn to field and back again each day. There was little danger of theft, for Maurice and Peter had, I learned, engraved their initials on the handles: MM and PM.

I could think of nothing better to do, so I stopped in the road to watch Maurice and Stephen fit the yoke to the oxen and then harness them to the plow. The docile beasts knew what was required of them, and awaited the command and goad. Maurice saw me watching the process and tugged a forelock. As did Stephen.

Adela and Janyn had made Stephen Parkin a grandfather. The man could be little older than me. Mayhap forty years or so. Likely even he did not know of a certainty. Years of poverty had left his beard white, his face deeply lined, and his thinning hair grizzled beneath his cap. But Stephen was not frail. He grasped the plowshares, shouted to the beasts as Maurice poked them with the goad, and away the team went, starting a new strip.

It is difficult to turn a team of oxen and a plow, so fields are not square, but long and narrow. I watched as men and oxen came to the end of the first furrow, some two hundred paces distant, then turn the beasts and plow in order to return. I watched, but my mind was elsewhere, considering how in the coming days I might succeed at what I had thus far failed to do, finding a felon and such.

I was about to turn away from Maurice and Stephen when I heard the latter yelp. Stephen leaped back from the plowshares and stumbled a dozen or so paces across the new furrow. I was curious as to what might have interrupted the work.

Maurice halted the oxen, then looked back at the plow, his face filled with concern.

The oxen, no longer feeling the goad, stopped in their tracks. Maurice looked to the edge of the field, walked rapidly to the hedgerow, and twisted a branch from a shrub. He then broke the bough into a "Y" shape. All this time Stephen stood frozen, gazing at the new-turned soil.

Maurice, his tool in hand, cautiously approached the plow. I stood at the hedgerow, curious as to what I was seeing. I watched as he carefully poked the broken branch toward the ground. He bent to the furrow and, whilst yet pressing the "Y" end of his stick to the ground, reached with his free hand and lifted a wriggling adder from the dirt.

The plow had burst through the snake's burrow and interrupted its winter slumber. Maurice had the adder grasped tightly behind its head. Stephen retreated further as Maurice held it out toward him.

Maurice had doubtless disturbed the occasional adder during late-winter plowing in years past. Whatever fear he felt, he was evidently determined to get the job done. He tossed the stick aside, strode across the fallow section of the field, and, when he came to the wooded verge, hurled the snake into the trees.

Stephen cautiously returned to the plow, uncertain as to whether or not adders might seek companionship of their kind in their winter sleep, and another might crawl from the furrow. He warily took his place between the plowshares, glancing about him all the while, and seemed relieved when Maurice retrieved the goad and the oxen leaned into the yoke.

No more adders appeared, and I had wasted enough time watching this affair unfold. I decided to seek William Lacy. He alone was alive of the three lads who had been friends. Was he in peril? Mayhap he knew something, as perhaps Thomas Rous had, which could place him in danger. And it could be that the lad did not yet know what he knew.

Philip Lacy, his wife said, was plowing in a field near to Cowley's Corner. William was there also, likely breaking clods with his bare feet. 'Twas not yet time for a plow team to stop their work to take dinner. If I hurried I could catch Philip and whoso was with him whilst they were yet at their labor.

As I expected, the lad was following the plow, stomping upon lumps of turf the plow had opened but occasionally not fully turned.

As I approached the end of a strip to meet Philip and his plow team mate, the noon Angelus rang from the distant tower of St. Beornwald's Church. This seemed to be a signal, as the two men and the lad stopped at the end of the strip, turned oxen and plow, then walked away toward the Weald.

I was suddenly hungry for my own dinner and worried about Kate's safety, so I decided to delay speaking to Philip Lacy and his lad until they returned to plow and oxen.

Chapter 9

Both of my concerns were soon alleviated. Kate was well, but becoming exasperated at being a prisoner in her own home. As 'twas a fast day, I did not expect something toothsome and was pleasantly surprised to find stockfish in bruit awaiting me. Kate had a small portion of salted stockfish remaining, so had been able to create something more palatable than a pea and bean pottage.

I explained my concern for William Lacy as we ate. "Two of the three lads Bessie named as friends are now dead. I believe I know why Kendrick Wroe was slain, if not who did the felony. But I have no idea why Thomas Rous was stabbed, and that ignorance causes me to worry that William Lacy may meet with an untimely death for the same unknown reason."

"There must be some great issue," Kate said, "for a man to slay two lads, possibly three, if your fears are founded."

"One would assume so," I said. "But mayhap Thomas's death was to obscure Kendrick's, and Kendrick's due to some small matter."

"Like poaching Lord Gilbert's fish?"

"Indeed. Some man slew Thomas, abducted Bessie and attacked you, all to hide his guilt for an insignificant violation. Men no longer have their eyes put out if caught poaching."

"And he may yet target the Lacy lad?"

"If he believes William knows of his perfidy."

"Does he?"

"When I spoke to William, he said not."

"He may fear what the felon would do if he were to learn that William had informed against him."

I heard Kate bar the door of Galen House as I departed for the field near to Cowley's Corner. Philip Lacy and his plow mate were there before me. But I did not see William with them.

The two men set the oxen to their work. I saw Philip look over his shoulder several times. Was he seeking his lad?

I stopped the plowmen at the end of a strip. They tugged their forelocks and looked at each other, as if both thought the other would know why I had halted them.

"Is William not assisting you this afternoon?" I asked.

"S'posed to be," Philip said. "Promised 'e'd be along. Child takes for ever to eat 'is dinner."

This must have been why Philip was looking over his shoulder as they plowed the first strip of the afternoon. The man's face was fixed in a glare. When he did arrive, William would receive a tongue-lashing.

The men and oxen plowed another strip, and still William did not appear. I began to worry. No lad would take an hour to eat his dinner. Lads of William's age are but an appetite with skin stretched around it.

Philip's brows lowered even further, but he did not leave the plow to search for William. I decided I would do so. In the distance I heard someone singing. Whoso made this music was too far away to identify, but the voice was pleasant.

There was a path between the Weald and the field being plowed, which led between hedgerows nearly as tall as me. This track was narrow and overgrown, and a lad as slight as William would be hidden 'til he emerged. Which he had not done.

I walked across the plowed portion of the field toward the opening to the path. Philip watched as he goaded the oxen, surely curious as to my purpose. Whoso had been singing stopped abruptly.

From the plowed field to the Lacy home in the Weald is about three hundred paces. I had walked about half that distance when I found William. He lay crumpled upon the brown, winter-killed weeds so that his brown cotehardie, cut down for him from one his father had discarded, blended with the foliage.

I ran the last few paces and bent over the child, fearing he was dead. I placed two fingers upon the lad's scrawny neck and felt a faint heartbeat. I saw red bruises which would soon be purple where some man's hands had throttled William.

Had I come upon the scene in time to prevent William's murder? Surely the man who had wrapped his hands about William's neck did not intend the lad to survive.

I had neither seen nor heard any man fleeing from the scene as I approached. Should I leave the child where he lay and run down the path to the Weald? Mayhap, if the rogue was not swift, I might catch him. William was alive and breathing, although unconscious. I called out for help, hoping that his father would hear and come to the boy's aid.

Then I stood and ran down the path toward the Weald. I am not so swift as I once was, Kate's cookery having much to do with my loss of speed. Kate's view is that a slender husband reflects badly upon his wife's culinary skills. She is not entirely accurate, for I have maintained the slender form of my youth, mostly, while Kate's cooking leaves nothing to be desired.

I broke from the overgrown path into the street and quickly glanced both ways. No man ran in the Weald. Whoso had tried to strangle William had outpaced me and was not in sight.

There was nothing to do but return to William to see if the lad had regained consciousness.

I hurried back along the path. About halfway to where William lay, I saw a place where the shrubbery of the hedgerow was snapped and splintered. In my haste a few moments before, I had not noticed the breakage. Should I plunge through the hedgerow? Had the man I chased done this? If so, he was well beyond pursuit. I returned to William.

There was a slight turn in the path, and when I rounded it I saw William sitting up, rubbing his abused neck. He saw me and, I think, assumed I was his assailant returning to finish the job. He tried to stand and run off, but his knees failed him and he fell to the sod. He tried to scramble through the hedgerow but was met with fists full of nettles, which quickly disabused him of the notion. He turned again to me and, perhaps because I was a few paces closer, he saw 'twas Lord Gilbert's bailiff who approached. Relief washed over his face.

William was clearly in no condition to walk to the plowed field, even with assistance. I gathered the lad in my arms, which, due to his frail physique, required no great feat of strength. William threw his arms about my neck, and thusly we passed from path to plowed field.

Philip saw us leave the path, threw down the goad, and ran to his son. As his father approached, William unclasped my neck and stumbled to Philip. I was pleased to see that he was able to remain vertical. Much asking and answering followed. The lad began to sway, and I told him to sit before he fell.

William did not know who had attacked him. The man had crept up behind him without his notice, he said. I thought this odd, considering how dry and winter-browned the weeds and grasses and twigs are in February, but I held my tongue and listened. An answer was forthcoming.

"Was you singin' again?" Philip asked.

"Aye," William whispered.

"Sings to 'isself, does William," Philip said with a shake of his head.

No wonder the lad had not heard the villain's approach. I thought it likely that William dreamed of entering a monastic house, where he could sing the canonical hours with brother monks. But for a lad with no coins to offer an abbot, such an arrangement was nigh on impossible. Mayhap when this business was over I would speak to Abbot Gerleys of Eynsham Abbey, as I had some influence with him. If William and Philip wished it.

I had thought to ask William earlier this day if he could shed any more light on the actions and deaths of Kendrick Wroe and Thomas Rous. I asked now, but he shook his head and, given his condition, I decided not to press the matter. Even had he known something, he would likely be too afraid now to share it, lest the felon return to finish the job.

My thoughts returned to the opening in the hedge. I began to wonder if the knave who tried to throttle William had passed through the hedgerow in two directions: once to come up behind the singing child, and again to escape my pursuit. I retraced my steps to the place.

The spot was blessedly free of nettles. Of course, had it not been, the scoundrel would likely have chosen some other place to penetrate the barrier. Even though the foliage was free of leaves, the twigs and branches were dense enough that I could not see past into the forest beyond. When I did finally clamber through, opening a seam in my cotehardie in the process, I found myself in a coppiced wood.

I walked perhaps three hundred paces into the forest, which was easy to do, as folk had gleaned fallen sticks and branches for winter fuel. There was nothing on the forest floor to trip a man but for the occasional limb which had fallen in the winter storms and not yet been collected.

The damp coating of leaves left no trail to follow. But I pressed on, searching for I knew not what. The farther I walked, the more familiar the wood seemed. No wonder. I came upon the tree to which Bessie had been bound. Would a felon return to the scene of his crime? It seemed a foolhardy thing to do. But if felons were wise they would not be felons. Probably.

I kicked through the leaves for five or so paces around the tree, but found nothing the other searchers had not already discovered.

Supper was a lonely meal. I missed Bessie's prattle, although I admit there are occasions when I would prefer that she eat as silently as John. I would soon discover that I was not the only person to think thusly.

"The page, Charles, brought a message," Kate said. "Lord Gilbert wishes you to call on him tomorrow."

I expected to find my employer warming himself in the solar, and so I did. I hoped that Lady Joan would not be present. In this respect I was disappointed. Indeed, she was the one who had prompted Lord Gilbert to send for me.

Lord Gilbert seemed hesitant to introduce the reason he had asked me to visit the castle. He began by asking of any progress in discovering the felon or felons who had slain Kendrick Wroe and Thomas Rous. I was forced to admit that there was none, then told him of the attempt on William Lacy's life, which I had been fortunate enough to frustrate. He nodded as I explained the conditions in Bampton, and raised one eyebrow as he is wont to do when perplexed. Lady Joan, as is her custom, frowned whilst I spoke.

"On to another matter," Lord Gilbert said, and I immediately understood that this "other matter" was the reason for my summons. "Bessie and John must return to Galen House." He glanced toward Lady Joan from the corner of his eye, and I saw her features change from displeasure to triumph.

"Why must this be?" I asked. "They will be like chicks in a hen coop, protected from a fox, but unable to leave it."

"Your Bessie jabbers endlessly at dinner."

As Bessie was the daughter of a knight, she was assigned a place at the high table. Was she, I wondered, seated beside Lady Joan? "Bessie," I said, "is an obedient lass. If you demand silence of her at table she will comply."

"And there is the matter of her reading my book of hours."

"If she is doing so against your will, command her to stop. Again, I know my Bessie. She is a curious lass but would not disobey you."

During most of my conversations with Lord Gilbert when Lady Joan was present, she was silent, looking on with either approval or disapproval. Usually disapproval. Now she spoke. "Charles bestows entirely too much attention upon your Bessie. And when he smiles at her she returns it with a silly grin. His mother sent him to his uncle to learn the manly arts, not to simper about after a maid far beneath his station. One who could bring him no wealth or land."

I could have argued the point about Bessie's station, but as to wealth and lands, she spoke the truth. As Charles de Burgh's mother is also named Lady Joan, this whole tale becomes confusing when put to parchment.

"Must I tell Bessie to frown when Charles smiles at her?"

Lord Gilbert had been silent during this last exchange. Now he found his voice.

"You say that your Bessie is obedient. Very well, I will tell her to keep silent at table. As to reading my book of hours, what harm can be done by that?" As he said this, he looked straight at Lady Joan, and for once I saw her drop her eyes.

"As for Charles smiling at Bessie, of course he would. They have become friends, and your Bessie is a pert lass. As to lands and wealth, he will inherit half of his deceased father's estate when he comes of age, and the whole of it when his mother dies. He has no need to marry to acquire a great estate.

"I have changed my mind," he continued. "Bessie and John may continue to reside in the castle until you have discovered a felon, or felons as may be, and 'tis safe for them to return to Galen House."

I breathed a sigh of relief and was determined to redouble my efforts to find the murderer. I was convinced the deaths of Kendrick and Thomas were done by the hand of one man, although if Lord Gilbert or Kate demanded why, I would be hard pressed to give a reason.

I had just observed a remarkable transformation in Lord Gilbert. From hen-pecked husband, he had become once more the lord of Bampton Castle. I did not for a moment believe Lady Joan would accept this modification of her status without a quarrel. I saw much discord in Lord Gilbert's future. Had he the mettle to stand against Lady Joan's opposition? Against a foeman wielding a sword, Lord Gilbert had few equals. A resolute female, however, was another matter.

I departed the solar feeling much relieved. A man's mind can encompass only so much. If I had not to worry about Bessie and John, I could set my wits to seeking a felon. Doubtless this was what the rogue wished to prevent when Bessie was seized and Kate attacked. I was newly determined that he would fail.

I returned to Galen House for my dinner to find that Kate had prepared cony in cevy. I was relieved and soon sated. I told her of the troubling conversation with Lord Gilbert and its agreeable conclusion whilst we ate. Gilbert is old enough that he has some teeth with which to chew adult food, and shows every indication that he will become a trencherman. Kate looked on her gluttonous son with approval. As did I. The child was in no danger of wasting away from lack of nourishment.

I heard the noon Angelus ring from St. Beornwald's tower and decided to attend. I was making no progress in solving the two murders. Mayhap the Lord Christ would direct my thoughts if I spent more time considering Him and less time pondering the evils men do. Of these He was certainly familiar and would perhaps show me the way if

I was attentive to His voice. He did, but not in a fashion I might have expected.

Most who attend the noon Angelus are advanced in years, and no longer able to labor in fields and workshops. They see the gates of pearl in their near future and wish to be prepared for the occasion.

Father Thomas was surely surprised to see me among the halt and the lame. When the devotional was finished he approached, a question in his eyes. As I rarely attended an Angelus he was justified in his curiosity.

"You are well met, Sir Hugh," he said. "Have you discovered yet who slew Kendrick and Thomas?"

"Nay. I am attending the devotional because all I have so far attempted has been in vain. I hoped that by attending the devotional my mind might clear and I would see the facts in a new light."

"And did your plan succeed?"

"Nay," I admitted.

"Perhaps," the priest said, there is a way to seek wisdom of the Lord Christ. Have you heard of *sortes biblicae*?"

"Biblical lots? Nay."

"There is precedent in Holy Writ," Father Thomas said. "A lot was cast to replace Judas, and the choice fell to Matthias. Men of old, when perplexed beyond understanding, would open the Gospels and, looking up to the altar, place a finger upon the open page. The verse to which the finger pointed was deemed to be a message from the Lord Christ."

"Have you seen this done?" I asked.

"Nay."

"Mayhap 'tis but an old wives' tale."

"So it may be. But that does not mean the Lord Christ cannot guide the opening of His book, or direct the movement of a man's finger, or show truth in the sayings of old wives."

"Indeed. Would you have me try this?"

"Why not? You have brought your wits to the search for a felon and discovered little. Mayhap the Lord Christ has a message for you."

"If so, I am willing to hear it."

The church was empty. All those who had attended the devotional had departed. Father Thomas led me to the altar and said, "Wait here." Then he went to the sacristy and a moment later returned with a bound volume of the four Gospels, artfully embellished. This he placed upon the altar.

"What should I do?" I asked.

"Look up to the crucifix and the suffering of the Lord Christ. Then, without casting down your eyes, open the Gospels and place a finger upon the open page. We will see if there is a message for you appropriate for the times."

I did as the priest suggested. When I looked to the page and verse, my breath caught in my throat.

Father Thomas glanced over my shoulder and read the verse. "'Tis the ninth chapter of the Gospel of Luke," he said. "The sixty-second verse. 'But Jesus said to him, "No one, having put his hand to the plow, and looking back, is fit for the kingdom of God."'"

"Is there plowing involved in these murders?" Father Thomas continued. "'Tis the season for that work."

"Aye, there are plowmen who I believe know things which would go far to solving two mysteries. But mayhap this verse my finger picked out is but coincidence."

"Hah!" Father Thomas scoffed. "I have heard you say that bailiffs do not believe in coincidence."

"Mayhap," I suggested, "the verse has nothing to do with plowing, but is rather a message to me that I must not lose heart in seeking clues which will define a murderer. Or perhaps the Lord Christ is pointing me to a plowman. I wish I could discern His intent."

"You want Him to do it all for you? He has provided a sign. He leaves you to carry on with the path He has pointed out. He must trust that you have the wit to do so."

"If so," I said, "the Lord Christ has more confidence in my wisdom than I do."

"Do not deprecate His direction. Mayhap He has pointed you in the direction you must go, and it is now your duty to follow the track."

"Which track?"

"To my mind," Father Thomas said, "the hint has to do with plowing fields."

"Not to my own persistence?"

The priest shrugged. "I am unwilling to set you on the wrong path. I tell you only my view, flawed as it may be. I am certain of but one thing. There is every reason to believe that the Lord Christ has given you a push in the direction He would have you go."

"Then I will seek the way He has set before me."

Chapter 10

The death of Peter Mainwaring was lodged in the back of my mind like a blackberry seed in a wisdom tooth. I had seen Stephen Parkin leap back when the plow he was wrestling with unearthed an adder. Somehow, another adder had bitten Peter whilst he was abed, and either it had done so before Margaret joined him in bed, or it had ignored her, to her great good fortune.

Maurice Motherby had also seemed alarmed, but had handled the snake with an experienced hand and confident demeanor. He struck me as a man who would not readily allow something as insignificant as an adder to thwart his plans.

Did the adder which struck Peter down slither unaided into his bed, or was it transported there by a man with some experience of dealing with snakes? No sooner had the thought occurred to me than I dismissed it. Why would Maurice want to slay his plow team mate? When I had last seen the two together they had been jovial. Until they saw me observing them; then their attitudes changed. What did that mean? Was I making something of nothing?

I tried to dismiss the thought, but could not. Since this was so, I decided to pursue it until I could make either something or nothing of the idea. Stephen Parkin could not have taken an adder to Peter Mainwaring's bed, unless he was a greater actor than I suspected, but he might know something of Maurice Motherby's opinion of his former plow mate.

The day was far gone, so 'twas likely Stephen and Maurice would have finished the day's work. I studied Galen House to assure myself that all was well as I walked past on my way to the Weald. I saw Stephen before me as I turned from Bridge Street into the Weald. My surmise had been correct.

I rapped upon the door through which Stephen had entered moments earlier. He opened it and tugged a forelock when he saw who stood before him. A cloud of smoke drifted out from inside the hovel. His wife was simmering pottage upon the hearthstone and the eave vents were not functioning well due to decayed thatch drooping over them. I had no wish to spend any time in the fumes and depart reeking. Kate would not welcome me if I fouled the scent of Galen House.

"Walk with me," I said to Stephen. "I will not keep you from your supper for long."

He looked sheepish but obliged.

"Yesterday you received a fright which drove you from the plowshares," I began. "The plow unearthed an adder, which Maurice bravely disposed of. What did he say of the creature after he hurled it into the wood?"

"'One less to trouble us,' as I remember."

"Nothing more?"

"I said somethin' 'bout why the Lord Christ would make such snakes, as they cause so much trouble for menfolk."

"Did he reply?"

"Aye. Didn't 'ear 'im clear, like, but 'e said somethin' 'bout adders bein' useful to catch rats an' mice an' such."

"Aye," I agreed.

"But there be snakes what catches mice what don't slay a man if they strike 'im. Seems to me the Lord Christ could've been satisfied with makin' just them snakes."

"Indeed," I agreed.

We passed Philip Lacy's house as we conversed. The man was carrying an armful of sticks into his house and nodded as we passed, intending to show respect for my station without the ability to tug a forelock. Loaded down as he was, I could not expect him to do so.

"Have you heard of the attack on William yesterday?" I asked Stephen.

"Aye. All the Weald be talkin' of it."

"What do folk say?"

"The lad must've angered someone, folk say. Although what 'e could've done to make someone so vexed, no one knows. William's a feeble lad, not likely to do aught to provoke anyone."

Our course took us to the end of the lane through the Weald.

"There have been reports of a young lady wandering down by Shill Brook in the small hours," I said. "Have you heard any such rumors?"

Stephen stopped in his tracks. When I raised my gaze, I saw that his face had reddened. Could he have engaged in a rendezvous with some young floozy before dawn? Might Kendrick have witnessed the meeting and threatened to reveal Parkin's guilty secret? Was it possible that Thomas and Peter also had knowledge of these romantic meetings?

"I . . . erm . . . No, sir. No such rumors 'ave reached me ears. But then I ain't much one for gossip."

I released Stephen to return to his smokey supper, then entered the wood where Bessie had been bound and where I had followed, as well as I could, the track of him who had tried to dispatch William Lacy.

I could not escape the thought - or the hope - that some object might be found near the tree where Bessie was bound which had evaded discovery even after two inspections. I circled the oak in widening spirals.

Night drew near. One last circumnavigation of the oak, six or so paces from the tree, and then I would turn toward home. Kate would worry was I not home when darkness enveloped Church View Street. She had enough to worry about. I must not add to her burden.

The rope was the same color as the winter foliage and damp leaves, so 'tis a wonder that, in the failing light, I saw it at all. Was this length of hempen cord used to bind Bessie? When the place of her confinement was first found there was no trace of the rope which had bound her, the rag which was her gag, the sack which covered her head, or the blindfold which hid her captor from her. 'Twas clear the felon had got to the place before we searchers and taken away all objects he feared might incriminate him. Had he, in haste, bungled the job and dropped or mislaid a length of hempen cord?

One hempen rope is much like another, and if this rope had any distinctive feature 'twas too dark to see it. I coiled the rope and set off for Galen House. I would inspect it in the morning, in the light of day.

I left the wooded area and turned toward Galen House. As I did so, I saw the retreating form of a young woman. I could not identify her from behind, and mayhap I could not have done after gazing on her face. Before I had gathered my wits enough to call out to her, she was gone. What business could she have had in the woods as darkness was beginning to fall? Might she have been there waiting for Stephen Parkin? When he did not appear, she would no doubt have wished to return to the place from whence she came without being seen.

I was beginning to give some credence to Gaston Miller's claim that a lass had been spotted down by Shill Brook whilst Kendrick Wroe was out wandering alone in the early hours. But was it Parkin she had gone to meet or some other fellow? I felt a deep sense of frustration rise within me. I was no closer to finding the killer than when I first discovered that Kendrick's death was no tragic accident.

As I expected, Kate had been anxious when darkness engulfed Church View Street and I had not returned home. She chided me for causing her worry, then led me to the kitchen where a kettle of pea and bean pottage simmered on the hearth. I was so late, and the pottage had cooked so long, that it was the consistency of hide glue. This was no fault of Kate's. My tardy appearance was the cause.

Kate spooned out a lump of pottage, set it before me, then noticed the length of rope I had coiled over my shoulder. I told her about my discovery of the rope near to the tree to which Bessie had been bound whilst I consumed my congealed supper. I also told her of the woman I had seen loitering near the woods, who had slipped away upon seeing me, and of Stephen Parkin's reddened face when I had mentioned such a woman.

That night I slept soundly, knowing my family to be safe in the castle and Galen House. When I awoke, the hempen cord rested where I had left it the evening before, reminding me that I wanted to closely inspect it.

I uncoiled and stretched it out upon the table. In the light of day, I saw that it was not whole. It was one strand of a three-strand rope. Undulating twists proved this. Extended upon our kitchen table, the rope was long enough that it doubled back upon itself. 'Twas about four paces long, mayhap a little more. If it had been used to bind Bessie, then lost or discarded, the felon evidently thought a single strand strong enough to secure a lass to a tree.

I had seen such a partial rope before. Kendrick Wroe's net had been made of the same stuff. How could this be? Kendrick was a corpse before Bessie was taken. He could not have tied her to an oak, and would have had no reason to do so even if he yet lived.

Had I been wrong about Kendrick? Was he not a poacher? Had he come upon some other man taking Lord Gilbert's fish and been slain to silence him?

If so, after making his net the poacher had presumably had a strand of rope remaining, of which he used some in his abduction of Bessie so as to silence me. Did he then, having failed to divert my pursuit, attack Kate, springing upon her in the dark, leaving behind a shoe which identified him as a man with a missing toe?

Had the poacher been involved in something even more untoward? I could not shake the image of the lass who had retreated from sight. Mayhap Kendrick had uncovered a romantic tryst and been dispatched by one of the lovers. Could Stephen Parkin be the killer?

Many questions, few answers. I have discovered in my various investigations that this is the nature of a bailiff's work. The deeper I go into the search for a felon, the more questions I uncover. As I bring light to these newfound issues, the resolution will suddenly appear. I hoped I was near to that point in the multiple matters now confronting me. I feared that if I did not soon find the felon I would be relieved of my bailiff duties, losing Galen House and the life I had built for my family in the process. Sir Gilbert had been patient so far, but he would not wait for ever for the murderer to be apprehended.

I had not discarded the net I found in Shill Brook. I retrieved it from the corner where I had, to Kate's consternation, tossed it. I had promised her I would dispose of it, or find some use for the cords, once this puzzle was solved. My Kate prefers an orderly house and labors mightily to keep Galen House so.

I brought the net to the table and compared its composition to the unraveled rope I had found in the wood. The two objects were much alike, which could, I suppose, be said of any two lengths of hempen cord. The most I could learn from placing the cords together was that they were not dissimilar.

Kate had been watching this exercise with interest. Now she spoke. "You have learned something, I think."

"Aye, but what it may be is uncertain. The net used to poach Lord Gilbert's fish and the unraveled cord I found in the forest which may have been used to bind Bessie perhaps come from the same whole rope before it was unraveled."

"Perhaps? Is there no way to be certain?"

"Not that I know of."

I placed the rope and net back into the corner from which I had extracted the net. Kate rolled her eyes.

If abducting Bessie and attacking Kate had been designed to distract me from the pursuit of the felon, his plan had failed. I should have considered what action the rogue might next attempt. I have, as my duties to Lord Gilbert require, often encountered evil men. One would think I might have become clever at predicting their motives and actions. Unfortunately, one would be wrong.

I spent the day fruitlessly. Plow teams were at work and needed no advice from me. I found myself studying men's shoes, seeking an unmatched pair on the feet of some man who might have lost a shoe. I saw none. Nor did I see any spare lengths of hempen rope lying about. Such an item, if it existed, would be coiled in a man's house, not on display hung on his latch.

Shortly after dark, as Kate and I prepared for bed, I heard Kate's hens clucking. Something had disturbed them. A fox, likely. I grabbed the poker from the fireplace, unbarred the kitchen door, and went out into the chilly night. An iron poker is a poor weapon against a quick fox, but I had nothing else ready to hand.

'Twas cloudy, moonless, and too dark to see a fox even if I had been fast enough to strike one before it could escape with a hen. As I approached the coop, the hens became silent. Whatever had alarmed them had apparently departed. Odd, I thought, that I'd heard only a general clucking from the hen coop but no noisy squawking of a fowl which had found itself in the jaws of a fox.

I stood in the dark, staring in the direction of the now silent coop. A troubling thought crossed my mind. What if there was no fox? What else might temporarily disturb a coop full of roosting hens? I grasped the iron poker and raised it above my head. Was some man prowling in the toft? If so, to what purpose?

If a man had seized a chicken and wrung its neck it could make no protesting squawk. The winter had been long and cold. Mayhap some man had crept into the toft, knowing my Kate keeps hens, and snatched a chicken to feed his bairns. Should I resent the loss? I lowered the poker and was about to return to the house when I heard what sounded like the snapping of a twig.

A man attempting to steal a chicken would not linger with his booty. Mayhap what I heard was the thief attempting to sneak away.

What if these suppositions, which flashed through my mind faster than I could write of them, were mistaken? Was there a man, perhaps clad in black so he would be invisible, standing behind the hen coop – silent now, watching for me? Had he rattled something against the hen coop so as to disturb the hens, knowing the uproar would draw me from Galen House?

Mayhap he hoped I would circle the hen coop, and had shifted his weight, causing him to step on a twig. If this were so, the fellow was not interested in a poultry dinner. He lay in wait for me.

I raised the poker again, then slowly backed toward the kitchen door. I opened the door – I really must grease the hinges – then closed it loudly whilst remaining outside, peering into the dark, listening.

I had not long to wait. I heard, then saw, a shadow appear beside the hen coop. Kate's hens are white, and may be glimpsed even on a dark night. The prowler had nothing white in his hand.

I opened the kitchen door again. The shadow stopped momentarily. Then, realizing he was found out, he ran. I heard heavy footfalls as the man darted around Galen House and disappeared down Church View Street. I assume he disappeared. I did not follow to see.

Kate stood silently when I entered the kitchen and then barred the door.

"A fox?" she said.

"Nay. A thief, or prowler."

"Come to steal a hen?"

"Aye, likely," I agreed.

But as we ascended the stairs to our bed, I vowed to myself that I would take care. Mayhap the felon I sought had decided that, if I could not be diverted from seeking him through threats to my family, I might be permanently halted with a dagger between my ribs or a cudgel laid across my skull.

I would not voice this concern to Kate. If she noticed my new caution and commented on it, I would not dissimulate. If she did not regard a change, which I would try to minimize, I would not cause her more worry than she already faced.

I rarely went about with my dagger, but decided I should begin to do so. Kate would see and wonder at it. This could not be helped, unless I confined myself to Galen House. How then could I find the felon? Some problems have many solutions, none of them good.

I wear a belt with my cotehardie, as do most younger men who have no paunch to hide. I thought I could obscure, at least partly, the fact that I had a dagger secured under the belt. This was a foolish endeavor. Kate saw and immediately divined my purpose.

"The prowler last night," she said, "took no hens, did he? I had sixteen. If you permit me to leave the house I will no doubt find that there are yet sixteen hens. And I need to gather their eggs. The dagger I now see under your belt will protect us while I do so."

Together we collected seven eggs, then opened the coop to allow the hens freedom to hunt and peck for the day. I had little fear for my safety in the day, but nevertheless the presence of the dagger on my hip lent a sense of security.

After breaking my fast with a maslin loaf and ale – stale, as neither Kate nor I had thought to visit Milicent Baker – I set out for the holy man's hut. I was so apprehensive that as I walked along Church View Street and past the castle, I imagined sinister figures lurking behind houses and barns and shrubs. Well, I think 'twas my imagination.

The holy man never seemed to bar his door, as he had little enough to steal, so I pushed it open and found him still abed. This was a good sign. Likely he had crept about Bampton's streets in the night, and this was the reason he was not eager to crawl from his warm bed at first light.

The door opening caused him to blink awake. He crawled out from under his blanket and prodded some embers on his hearthstone to life.

I waited until he had placed fresh sticks on the smoldering ashes, then spoke. "Did you walk Bampton's streets last night?"

He nodded.

"Did you enter Church View Street?"

Another nod.

"Did you see a man run from Galen House?"

He raised his hands, palms up, to indicate confusion.

"You saw a man on Church View Street, and running, but you did not see him enter the street from Galen House or the toft?"

He nodded.

"Did you follow?"

The holy man shook his head.

"Did he run too fast for you to pursue?"

Another nod.

I wondered where the runner had been when the holy man lost sight of him in the dark. After several more questions, nods, and shakes, I learned that the man who had fled Church View Street turned left onto the High Street, and after that he disappeared.

This meant that, unless he purposely took a roundabout path to his home, he did not reside in the Weald.

"Will you be upon Bampton's streets again this night?" I asked.

He nodded.

"Pay particular attention to Galen House. If you see a secretive fellow breaking curfew, rap on the door of Galen House, and if I see 'tis you I will know why you seek me."

The holy man nodded again.

"It may be that the man you saw dashing down Church View Street will not appear again for several nights. Will you do me this service each night for the next week?"

The holy man nodded. Vigorously. I believe he enjoyed being useful in such secretive matters. I would also speak to John Whitestaff. With him and the holy man keeping watch on Galen House, and a dagger tucked into my belt, I felt reasonably secure.

Chapter 11

As 'twas a fast day, Kate could not prepare a dinner which included fresh eggs. Perhaps Sunday I might enjoy an egg leach. Our dinner this day was a simple pottage of peas and beans, the same meal most of Bampton would consume, except for those in the castle. Bessie and John, I reflected, seated at the high table as befitted their station, would enjoy fish and other permitted delicacies. Neither pea nor bean would likely sully their trenchers.

Sunday evening, about an hour past sunset, the holy man came knocking upon the door of Galen House.

I had been reading my Bible by candlelight – translating for Kate as I read, as she has no Latin – from the fourth chapter of Proverbs. "Do not enter the path of the wicked, and do not walk in the way of evil." There is much wisdom in the book. I find it profitable to consider what the ancient men of God have bequeathed to us.

The holy man's knuckles upon the door were so light I barely heard. When I did, I knew what the sound portended. Some man was on the street after curfew, and probably close by, else the holy man would not have thought it necessary to rap so faintly.

If I opened the door with the candle yet burning, the light, faint as it would be, would illuminate the opening door. I blew out the flame, leaving us in the dark, then went to the door and opened it. The front door hinges do not squeal.

There remained some pale twilight in the western sky. Enough that I could see, when I opened the door, the holy man point in the direction of the High Street. Try as I might, I could see nothing. My eyes, accustomed to the candlelight, were temporarily unsuited to peering into the dark.

Nevertheless, trusting the holy man's guidance, I set off down Church View Street at a trot, attempting a compromise between speed and silence. This was a failure. I saw movement in the fading light. Rapid movement. My pace was much too slow to catch the shadowy apparition.

I began to run, and as I did so the obscure runner vanished. This startling development was immediately followed by a curse. The man I pursued had evidently fallen, which had caused him to seemingly disappear. I vaguely saw him regain his feet and continue, but, it seemed to me, more slowly.

A moment later I learned why the man I pursued had fallen, when I did also. Winter rains had eroded a shallow trench across Church View Street. In the day this was no obstacle. Indeed, I had seen the trough many times and knew it was there. But I forgot. I plunged headlong into the mud.

I suffered no injury, but by the time I had hoisted myself from the mire, my quarry was gone. 'Twas the same man, I was sure, who but two days past had disappeared down the High Street. I had lost him again.

The holy man awaited me beside the door of Galen House. As 'twas now fully dark he could not see the sorry state of my clothing. I thanked him for his alert presence, admitted that the man I sought had eluded me again, and dismissed him.

Kate awaited my return in the dark kitchen. When she heard me speak to the holy man, she relighted the candle and was properly dismayed at my muddied appearance.

I have a half-barrel which I keep for bathing, but February is much too cold for its use. Kate heated a pot of water on a rekindled hearth and, with a patch of shrunken wool, I mopped the mire from face, hands, arms, and hair. My kirtle and braes could be properly laundered, but a woolen cotehardie is not so easy to deal with. There was nothing to be done but allow the garment to dry, then, in a few days, beat the dirt from it. After laundering it will shrink, and be suitable for John. Fortunately, I owned three other cotehardies.

Monday dawned fair and clear. A harbinger of spring after a long, cold, miserable winter. A good day for plowing. Men who had begun this work at Candlemas when their fingers were cold and numb on the plowshare would be pleased at the change.

Having failed twice to apprehend the man who lurked about Galen House, I had nothing better to do this day than amble through the town, hoping as I did so that some fresh idea would come to me regarding men who skulked in the dark and others who attacked lads who may have poached fish or witnessed an assignation, and whether or not these scoundrels might be one and the same.

I passed the field in which Maurice Motherby and Stephen Parkin had nearly completed plowing. There was no activity. The plow stood immobile at the end of a furrow, ready for the oxen and a new day. But there were no oxen and no men. This, I thought, was odd. Being so near to finishing their work, I had assumed Maurice and Stephen would be early to the field on such an agreeable morning.

I walked past Janyn Wagge's forge and heard the rhythmic clang of his hammer as he created some useful object. The door was open, and I peered in as I passed. I saw Stephen Parkin within, both hands gripping tongs whilst his son-in-law pounded the red-hot iron.

Stephen's presence in Janyn's smithy explained why he was not between the plowshares. Or did it? If Maurice wanted to finish plowing, and was paying Stephen to assist, then it must be that Maurice had some other obligation this day which had interfered with plowing.

This was not unusual. Plowing was the most important work at this time of year, but there were other duties which called men from the plowshares. Maurice, for example, had been on his way to collect fallen wood when he found Kendrick Wroe.

Janyn saw me looking through his open door and grinned. Having no other pressing duty, I entered to pass the time of day. Janyn rested the cooling iron upon which he was working on the embers and pumped the bellows. Flames sprang immediately to encompass the iron and it was soon glowing red again.

"You are not plowing today?" I said to Stephen.

"Nay. Maurice be ill, so 'is wife do say. 'E didn't come to the plow this mornin', so I went to 'is house. Janyn needed help, so 'ere I am."

The next few days passed with warming temperatures. There was no more morning ice on the mill pond, although it would be several months before the lads would gambol in Shill Brook. All these days Kate stayed within Galen

House and I ventured out only in the day, with my dagger tucked in my belt.

'Twas Thursday before I again saw Maurice and Stephen at work finishing their plowing. Stephen wrestled with the plow whilst Maurice jabbed at the oxen with the goad. It occurred to me that whenever I saw the two at work, Stephen was always between the plowshares and Maurice plied the goad. Stephen had by far the more exhausting labor, but I suppose he who pays the piper calls the tune.

Lord Gilbert's demesne lands were also being plowed, and John Prudhomme, Bampton's reeve, was observing the villeins whose work week involved the care of Lord Gilbert's fields. Lord Gilbert, like most of his rank, has decided that 'tis more profitable to rent his land to tenants than to hold men in villeinage. So John has little to do, and I suspect in another decade Bampton will have only tenants.

I was walking near to Cowley's Corner when I heard my name shouted in the distance. 'Twas Charles de Burgh, and I noticed as he called my name that his voice was changing from tenor to a manly rumble. I turned and met the lad not far from the path to the holy man's hut.

"Sir Hugh," the page said breathlessly, "m'lord would have you attend him at the marshalsea. Bucephalus has kicked a groom and injured him grievously."

The dexter was, I knew, a bad-tempered beast, as are many stallions; even runcies and amblers and such. Many knights pride themselves on the vicious nature of their war horses. Their ability to control such a beast is a mark of manliness, and 'tis assumed that an ill-natured beast will be more willing to charge into battle, even if wounded.

I hurried behind Charles to the castle, thence to the row of stables. A crowd had gathered around the injured man. Bessie and John were among the onlookers. Lord Gilbert knelt over the prostrate groom and Lady Joan looked on. Frowning. No doubt she thought the groom's injury his own fault for being careless around the malicious animal.

I knelt beside Lord Gilbert and he spoke. "This injury is much like the one I suffered on the street in Oxford, when you sewed up my leg."

"Similar," I agreed, "but not the same. The gash in this fellow's leg is small, but the bone is clearly broken. See how askew it lies. I must return to Galen House for some herbs which will dull this man's pain, for linen strips and reeds, and for a needle and silk thread. Have a cup of ale ready upon my return into which I can place the herbs, and also wine to bathe the laceration. What is the man's name?"

"I'm Bartholomew, but folk do call me Bart," the injured man said. "Can you mend me leg?"

"Aye, but before I can, I must get the proper implements. Try to remain still meanwhile. I will return anon."

As I departed the stable, I saw that Bessie was standing beside Charles. Well, she had to stand somewhere, I supposed. Or was it Charles who stood beside Bessie?

I expected the door to Galen House to be barred, with Kate safe inside, so I rapped firmly and called out so that she would hear my voice. No doubt she was busy preparing my dinner. In a manner of speaking, she was.

I stood before the door, shifting my weight from one foot to the other, impatient to gather needle, thread, linen strips, and reeds. When Kate did not soon appear, fear clutched at my heart and I pounded again upon the door. Vigorously.

When Kate still did not appear, I ran around the house to try the kitchen door. I found it open, and my heart skipped a beat.

"Kate!" I yelled.

"Here I am," she said calmly, emerging from the hen coop with a basket of eggs. I was too relieved to see her safe to scold her for leaving the house, but she knew my thoughts – I've always wondered how she does that – and said, "If you want a dinner, I must gather the makings of it. I am safe here in the day, when if some man attacks I can scream for help. Besides, I am armed."

She held out one of my largest scalpels, made of the finest Toledo steel, with a keen edge which could gut a hog in a trice. Indeed, in the hands of a determined belligerent it could be as deadly as a dagger. Would Kate be so determined? I asked the question.

"I wish to see Bessie and John and Gilbert grow and have babes of their own. I would not be pleased to slay a man, but I believe I have the pluck to wound a man grievously if he dared try to send me to the churchyard."

I know my Kate. I believed her.

I had no time to await my dinner, and it would take Kate some while to prepare the viand de leach she had planned. I explained the reason for my haste as I gathered the supplies I needed, told Kate to bar both doors until my return, then hurried off to the castle.

Why is it, I wonder, that other men's misery will attract a swarm of onlookers? Mayhap 'tis because they are pleased that some other man is suffering, and not themselves. Whatever the reason, the throng in the stable had increased 'til every member of the castle staff, even the cooks and scullery maids, had left off their other duties to observe my work. Lady Joan would not be pleased that her dinner would likely be delayed.

The crowd parted to allow me access to the injured man. The cup of ale I had requested was ready, as was the wine. Into the ale I mixed crushed hemp seeds and the powdered sap of lettuce. Bart did not need to be coerced to drink the potion. Most men will gladly imbibe their lord's ale, it being likely the brew is both fresh and unwatered.

It has been my experience that the use of hemp seeds and lettuce sap will be most effective in reducing pain an hour or so after the concoction is consumed. Thus, for two reasons I would attend the gash in the man's leg first: I could not stitch a cut if 'twas covered with linen strips and stiffening reeds; and the sting of a needle would not be so great as the hurt which comes when the broken ends of a bone are manipulated so as to join and thence knit properly.

I first bathed the cut in wine. A wound so cleansed will heal more readily, though no man knows why. Bart bore the prick of the needle well. As the laceration was in a place between knee and hip, but closer to his knee, where others were unlikely to see the scar, I used but five stitches to close the wound. More sutures, placed close together, will leave a less noticeable scar, but what would be the point?

When the wound was closed I bathed it again with wine, as there was some remaining. Bart looked on with an expression which said that he would rather have drunk the wine than see it mopped over his leg.

Partway through this work, Lady Joan elbowed her way past the other onlookers and departed the scene.

I last saw her climbing the outside stairs to the solar, clutching her stomach.

A few others also began to drift away. Apparently, they thought the excitement past. I hoped they were correct. If I could gently nudge the ends of the broken femur together, and the hemp and lettuce were effective, Bart would not loudly proclaim his agony but would bear the manipulation silently. Where is the excitement in that?

A man's thigh is a thick mass of flesh. I could see from its crooked shape that the femur was broken, but finding and fitting the fractured ends together would be a difficult task. Bart was not a frail man; his thigh was muscular. The kick which shattered his leg must have been mighty.

Delay would do Bart no good. The sooner he suffered the pain of having his fractured leg aligned, the sooner he would begin to heal. I set the reeds and linen strips beside the leg, ready at hand for when I had the appendage properly straightened. I then grasped Bart's thigh just above his knee and manipulated the broken end to put it straight.

Hemp seeds and powdered lettuce sap are the best weapons in my arsenal to fight pain. But even these often fail. When I pulled on his leg Bart gasped, his eyes rolled back in his head, and he swooned.

Here was nature's own relief from pain, and more efficacious than any herbs I could administer. Whilst he was unconscious I could work with little fear that I would cause Bart to jerk or writhe in pain and undo my labor. I went immediately to a final shifting of the bones, which caused Bart to twitch as the pain penetrated his dulled brain, and, with a final squeeze of the flesh, felt certain I had been successful in bringing the fractured ends together. Other than the minor twitch, Bart remained supine and senseless.

I placed the reeds – ten, to be sure of the stiffness – about the leg, then tied the linen strips securely about the reeds. Bart must not attempt to walk or support himself upon the leg for a month, I told Lord Gilbert. The castle carpenter must make a crutch for the fellow so that when necessity required it, he could leave his bed. Meanwhile, while he was yet insensible, it would be best to place him on a pallet and carry him to his bed.

John Chamberlain heard this advice. Lord Gilbert motioned to him, and John called four grooms to do as I had suggested. Bart's care was now in the Lord Christ's hands, no longer mine. Onlookers understood this, and those who had remained wandered away.

I stretched, my back aching from bending over the injured groom. Mayhap I should consume some of the crushed hemp seeds myself.

Chapter 12

My dinner awaited when I reached Galen House. As we ate, I told Kate of Bart and my treatment of his injury.

"Will he walk again?" she asked.

"If he stays abed as much as he can. He will require help to visit the garderobe. I surrounded his leg with plenty of sturdy reeds, so I am confident that he will walk again. But not soon."

After my dinner, I decided to seek the castle once more. Mayhap Bart had awakened from his swoon. My route through Bampton took me past the field where Maurice and Stephen were undertaking their labor. They had one furrow to complete, and I saw Maurice limp as he prodded the oxen to make the turn. Likely he had sprained an ankle, stumbling in a furrow.

At the castle, I sought the grooms' chamber, where these workers lived together like monks in a dortoir. The groom was awake, resting quietly, and indicated little pain when asked.

"Only when I shift meself," he said, "so I try not to."

"That would be best," I agreed. "If your pain increases, I will bring herbs which may reduce it and help you to sleep. My supply is small until next season's yield, so if you are not in great discomfort I will not make up potions."

"Ain't too bad," he said. "I can cope."

"I have asked Lord Gilbert to have a crutch made for you, so when 'tis necessary for you to leave your bed you will have support. Otherwise pain, for the next few weeks, will be your friend."

"Me friend? 'Ow so? Seems to me should be t'other way round. Pain be a foe."

"Pain is your body's way of telling you that you must stop whatever you are doing which caused the hurt."

"Ah . . . I see. You may trust me to keep from such, then."

For several hours my attention had been directed toward treating the injured groom. I had given no thought to Kendrick or Thomas. I appreciated the respite, but 'twas time to return to thoughts of felonies. Men are wicked creatures, prone to evil when villainy seems likely to be profitable. If men were by nature virtuous, what need then for the Lord Christ to die on a cross to expiate men's sins?

William Lacy, so far as I knew, was hale and healthy. No additional attempts had been made on his life or I would have been told. Nevertheless, I decided to call upon the family and enquire of any untoward events which might mean some man yet sought the lad's life.

Philip, his wife said, was with his plow team, as was William. Since the attack on their son, she added, Philip would not allow the lad out of his sight.

From the house I went to the field where Philip and his mate were at work. William was following behind the plow, breaking clods with his bare feet, and I saw that Stephen Parkin had joined Philip and his companion. Stephen had completed his work with Maurice and was now free to seek other employment. This addition would probably not speed the completion of the plowing, which was nearly accomplished anyway, but would allow for three men to take a turn between the plow handles, rather than two. This was work with which Stephen was familiar, having been assigned that duty by Maurice Motherby. But now two others shared the arduous work. Stephen, I knew, being a poor cotter, sought employment wherever it was to be found. When this strip was plowed, where would he next find work? For me, this was only a question. For Stephen and his family 'twas a full belly or empty.

I approached Philip Lacy and asked if any suspicious fellow had been lurking about the Weald or the field where he had been at work since Candlemas.

"Nay. An' I been keepin' a sharp eye out for such folk."

"Your wife said you keep William near you at all times."

"Aye. So I do. Why d'you suppose some fellow tried to throttle 'im?"

"Because," I said, "that man believes he knows something of the deaths of Kendrick Wroe and Thomas Rous."

"Bah. Did 'e, he'd share it with me."

"It may be that he does not know what he knows."

"Eh?"

"He may be ignorant of some fact which, if I knew it, would lead me to the murderer."

"You sayin' me son be ignorant?" he bristled.

"Nay. No man, nor boy, knows all. We are all ignorant on some matter or other. For example, can you shoe a horse?"

"Seen it done."

"Or set a man's broken leg?"

"Seen you do it."

"Not what I asked. Can you *do* these things?"

"Nay," he admitted.

"So it is with William. He is a simple lad, and would not dissemble, but someone believes he knows something of Kendrick's and Thomas's deaths, and wants to slay him before he becomes aware of his dangerous knowledge and tells others of it . . . tells *me* of it."

Stephen Parkin had overheard this conversation. "Mayhap," he said, "William ain't the only one 'ereabouts what knows somethin' what could get 'im slain."

I looked intently at Stephen and saw that he was serious. "What do you know which worries you?" I said.

"Rather not say. Just thinkin' out loud, so to speak. Prob'ly nothin', and did I speak of it, them who I spoke of would be . . ." He hesitated.

"Would be what?" I said.

"Wouldn't be happy. I'll say that much."

So Stephen Parkin may know something of the deaths of Kendrick and Thomas, of Bessie's abduction, and mayhap of other hidden matters? Or believes he does. Fears he does.

Was there one man of Bampton who had dealings with Kendrick, Thomas, William, Stephen, Peter, and even Bessie? Perhaps, taken separately, some of these matters might be viewed as benign, but together they might lead me to a felon. As I considered this, one name kept coming back to me. Conjecture, however, is not evidence.

Perhaps in the salubrious environment of Galen House I might ponder the names, and guilt might appear in my mind's eye.

I found Kate in tears, clutching Gilbert to her bosom. Few things will raise the ire of a man more than another who drives his wife to tears. My temper was instantly provoked, and I found another reason to apprehend the felon I sought.

"Will I ever be able to leave Galen House safely?" she sobbed. "Will Bessie and John be able to return home? Must I go about with your scalpel always at hand?"

She did not mean it so, I'm sure, but here was an indictment of my lack of success at finding a felon. Her weeping cut me to my heart and further deepened my resolve. But I must not, I thought, allow Kate's sorrow to influence my consideration of evidence. This would not be easy.

I did not wish to allow my desire to end the search for a felon, my desire to assuage her fears, cause me to charge the wrong man with the crimes which had plagued Bampton. In all my years of service to Lord Gilbert as bailiff of Bampton, I had never accused an innocent man of felony, and would not begin now. Although, in truth, I have come near to accusing the blameless once or twice, I restrained myself 'til more facts altered my opinion. A bailiff must deal with facts, not opinion.

Two weeks or so past I had suspected a man of slaying Kendrick Wroe but dismissed the thought as a product of opinion, not fact. Events, to be sure, had led to the opinion, and events can be construed as facts. Where did that leave me? Should I revisit my earlier opinion and see if more recent facts might suit it? Might facts be bent to fit a desired outcome?

Of course not, if I made sure to be honest. If my pursuit of a felon or felons was restricted to facts which resisted bending to agree with perception, which facts remained? Precious few. I wondered what Stephen Parkin thought he knew. Did it relate to the murders? To Bessie's abduction? To the mysterious lass Gaston Miller had mentioned and

I had seen loitering where she had no business to be, perhaps with a view to meeting Parkin himself?

I considered the few facts at my disposal as I rested my head on the pillow Thursday evening. I was comforted that Kate seemed recovered from her distress and slept. A long night of rest may solve some problems, though not all. Trouble which afflicts one at dusk generally remains at dawn. But not always.

I scratched my head as I lay abed, as if so doing would bring solutions to the surface. Doing this reminded me that my once curly and flourishing locks were now thinning. Does the Lord Christ smile to see hair growing from my ears whilst it stops covering my pate? He should have something to smile about, as men give Him enough reason for sorrow.

A waxing moon provided pale light to our chamber window about midnight. Slumber yet escaped me, which is why I heard the soft tapping upon the door of Galen House. I thought I knew who sought my attention, but nevertheless seized my dagger before I descended the steps to the hall and front door. Mayhap I had become excessively wary.

'Twas the holy man, as I had guessed. Something he had seen or heard he deemed important enough that even in the middle of the night I should know of it.

Before I could ask, he pointed down Church View Street toward the High Street, and motioned that I should follow. Moonlight glinted from my dagger and he stepped back, puzzled. I assured him he was in no danger, asked him to wait whilst I donned my cotehardie, then climbed the stairs to our bedchamber.

Gilbert had awakened, probably due to the combination of my rising from bed and an empty stomach. Although

Kate had been sound asleep, Gilbert shifting in his bed brought her awake. She was, like all mothers, instantly alert to any nocturnal behavior of her child.

She looked to my empty side of the bed, then saw me in the weak light from a rising moon at the head of the stairs.

"'Tis the holy man," I said before she could voice a question. "He wishes me to accompany him. I will have my dagger."

I could see that this announcement did not reassure Kate. But what could I do? I hurriedly drew on my cotehardie, cinched the belt, inserted the dagger, and clattered down the stairs before Kate could think of any reason to protest my prowling Church View Street in the night.

The holy man customarily wore garments others had cast off, usually of coarse wool, tending to dark brown and grey. So I had to blink twice before I saw him awaiting me in the shadows left by the ascending moon.

"Where are we going?" I said.

He again pointed down Church View Street, then set off. I followed.

We crossed the bridge over Shill Brook and then turned into the Weald. All was quiet, as it should be in the middle of the night. Yet there had to be some reason the holy man had sought me at such an hour.

I stopped in the lane, put a hand on the holy man's arm, and we both halted. I moved to the verge, in the shadow of some leafless shrubbery, and whispered, "Have you seen some man out here in the Weald after curfew?"

He nodded.

"Was he intent on some destination?"

He shook his head.

"Did he loiter in one place?"

Another nod.

"Did you see him skulking about some house?"

Another nod.

"Show me," I whispered, then placed a finger to my lips to urge silence. Maybe an unnecessary act when a man cannot speak. But footsteps can make sounds also. With the other hand I grasped the hilt of my dagger. I had promised Kate I would take care.

The holy man crept quietly from one shadow to another. I followed. He eventually halted before a house which I recognized as that of Philip Lacy.

"This is where the man you saw hesitated?" I whispered.

A nod.

Why would some man stand in the dark and watch a poor man's house? More specifically, why this house? Did someone dwell within who was of interest to some rogue? Indeed. William Lacy was within. But he was not likely to leave his bed and house in the dead of night. Was there another reason for the curfew-breaker's interest in the hovel?

There was. I saw a brief spark, then another. These were faint, but on a dark night seemed as bright as lightning. After the second spark I saw a flame, as from a candle, illuminate a man's cupped hands. Whoso had created the sparks wished to conceal the tender flame and nurture its growth. A moment later I saw the flame applied to a twist of dried reeds from the nearby brook. This produced enough light that I might have recognized the fellow, but he wore a cowl, like a monk's, which obscured his face.

I knew immediately his intention. He would toss the flaming reeds onto the thatching of Philip and Margery Lacy's hovel, and burn the dwelling whilst the family slept.

Before the rogue could set the thatching alight, I shouted, "Halt!"

The fellow dropped the burning reeds, looked about to see from whence the demand had come, then disappeared toward the stub end of the Weald. If he had not cast down the flaming rushes, the glow might have illuminated his face. But he did, so I was unable to see clearly who sought to burn a whole family in order to slay one member. This was, I was sure, an attempt to silence William. Some man of Bampton was becoming very fearful. A frightened man might do unpredictable things. I must be even more on my guard.

I did not pursue the scoundrel. I'd had enough of chasing malefactors down dark streets. If I had I might have caught him, but I did not know this 'til later.

My shout had awakened Philip. Well, it had probably awakened the entire family, but 'twas Philip who opened the door and peered out into the moonlit night.

"Who's there?" he bellowed.

"'Tis Sir Hugh," I replied.

"What d'you want? Why go about wakin' a man from 'is sleep?"

His eyes fell upon the still-glowing rushes and he fell silent, trying to understand the appearance of Lord Gilbert's bailiff in company with a mound of smoldering vegetation at his door, and what the relationship between the two might be.

He evidently failed in this undertaking. He stared silently from me to the rushes and back again.

I enlightened him. "Some man has tried to burn your house."

"Who?"

"I do not know. He ran off when I shouted. 'Twas the

holy man here who first saw him lurking about your house and came to me with the information. It is to him you owe your life."

"Why'd some man want to burn me 'ouse?" Philip muttered.

"To slay William. He did not care who else might die, so long as William perished. I told you before that the lad's life is in danger."

"You said 'e knows somethin', but 'e don't know 'e knows it."

"Aye. And the man who slew Kendrick and Thomas is likely the man who just now tried to burn your house. He fears that William will think on the deaths of Kendrick and Thomas, and that the hidden knowledge will suddenly become clear to him."

"What am I to do? Can't stay awake all night waitin' for the scoundrel to return."

"I doubt he will. At least, not with the same intent. But he will surely try some other way to silence William. The lad must be sent out of harm's way."

"Where?"

"Go back to your bed. I believe the danger is past for tonight. Meanwhile, I have an idea as to how William can be protected."

Bessie and John were protected in Bampton Castle, but their father was a knight. Lady Joan would surely put her foot down if Lord Gilbert accepted a cotter's lad as a castle resident. Even as a page. And I doubted Lord Gilbert himself would agree. It would be felt that Philip Lacy was the bishop's tenant, so let him look to the lad's safety.

The Bishop of Exeter was not near to take a hand in the matter. Responsibility would devolve upon the vicars of St. Beornwald's Church. They would be appalled at the attempts made on William's life, but what could they do about it? He was too young and uneducated to serve as a clerk, or even as an assistant to a clerk.

But the lad could sing, so his father said, and I had heard him distantly. How might that talent be of use where he would be safe from the man who wished to do him harm?

Abbot Gerleys of Eynsham Abbey was a friend of mine. I had done him good service some years past. Mayhap he would return the favor. William was unlettered, 'twas true, but might be teachable, and even if he never became literate enough to be a copyist, his voice might be added to the monks' when they sang the canonical hours.

Failing those possibilities, William might become a lay brother. Abbot Gerleys could choose. What was important was that the lad be got away from Bampton and the Weald. Soon.

Friday morning I broke my fast with a maslin loaf and a cup of stale ale, tucked my dagger into my belt, and sought the castle. I was off to Eynsham, and needed a palfrey from the castle marshalsea. I explained my purpose to Kate, and told her that I would return before dark. This assurance did not placate her. She did not want me to be upon a deserted road alone, where few would be near to hear me if I called out for help.

She had a point. The roads are not safe. Kate made me promise that I would ask Sir Jaket to accompany me.

The day had dawned bright and clear. Had there been a cold rain, the knight and his squire might not have wished to venture from the castle. But the roads were dry, the sun shone, and so, with Lord Gilbert's permission, Sir

Jaket and Thomas accompanied me under the portcullis and over the castle drawbridge at the second hour.

We arrived at Eynsham Abbey well before noon. 'Twas a fast day, but this made no difference, as Benedictines eschew meat. The rule says it must be so, although flesh is permitted in the misericord for brothers who are weak or ill. Because this proscription is so often ignored, the Cistercian Order came to be.

The abbey monks had just celebrated terce when we arrived. The porter at Eynsham was an elderly monk who was too frail to work and whose eyes were too weak to be a copyist. But his memory was good. He recognized my name, and when I told him I had business with Abbot Gerleys he sent a novice to seek the abbot.

Abbot Gerleys greeted me warmly. I had done the abbey good service when I discovered a heresy promulgated by his prior eleven years past. For his error, the prior was transferred to an abbey in Scotland, where he would regret his apostasy as each winter brought more aches to his bones.

At that time Abbot Gerleys had been novice master, with no desire to replace the aged abbot who administered the abbey. Because of his experience with lads, I thought Abbot Gerleys might be amenable to my request.

"What brings you to Eynsham?" the abbot asked, eying Sir Jaket and Thomas.

I introduced my companions. "I have an urgent request," I said, "which may involve a matter of life or death."

"Come to my chamber and tell me of it."

Once we were seated in his chamber, the abbot urged me to begin.

"There is a lad of Bampton whose life is in danger," I said. "Two attempts have already been made to slay him."

"A lad? Who would want to slay a youth?"

"A man who has already slain others: two youths and possibly a grown man."

"You suspect you know who has done these murders?"

"Suspect? Aye. But evidence is thin, and I can bring no charge against the man to the King's Eyre with the proofs I have collected."

"Is there something you want of me? Of course. Foolish question. You would not have traveled here from Bampton were there not a service I could render."

"The lad in danger is a poor cotter's son, a tenant of the Bishop of Exeter in the Weald, which you may know adjoins Bampton Manor and the lands of Lord Gilbert Talbot. Such a lad has no coins with which to provide for himself a place in a monastic house."

"You want me to allow this youth to enter Eynsham Abbey as a novice?"

"He sings well," I said.

"But a cotter's son will have no Latin," the abbot replied. "He'll not likely even read or write his own tongue. Choir monks must do more than sing the canonical hours."

"True," I admitted. "He'll not serve as a copyist. Although he seems quick-witted, and perhaps might be taught to read and write. But my purpose in coming here is to find a place for the lad where he will be safe, far from Bampton."

"I do not understand why the youth is in danger," Abbot Gerleys said.

"Neither does he, nor his father. I believe he knows something of the murders in Bampton, but does not understand the importance of what he knows."

So you want to get him away from some man who would slay him before he becomes aware of his danger?"

"William is aware of his danger. However, he does not know what he might know to cause the danger. If you will allow him a place here at Eynsham, he will be safe until I can prove the guilt of the felon who has already killed and would kill again."

"This sanctuary would be temporary, then?"

"Aye, unless he might remain to become a lay brother when he is older."

"If he sings well," the abbot mused, "he might memorize the hours, and of course he would hear each day a reading from the rule in the chapter house."

"Most important is that no one other than the monks and lay brothers of the abbey know he is here."

"You think the scoundrel who seeks his life might pursue him here if he knew of the lad's whereabouts?"

"Folk of the town are permitted to attend when the hours are sung. How many usually do?" I asked.

"A dozen or so," Abbot Gerleys replied. "Generally older folk, too frail to work."

"Would you recognize a stranger?"

"Probably. But I see your point. If a man knew that the lad – William, is it? – was here, he might devise some way to do him harm."

"Just so. Will you accept the lad?"

"Aye. When should I expect him?"

"Tonight. The sooner he is away from Bampton the better. Sir Jaket, Thomas, will you agree to bring him?"

Even an armed knight might hesitate to travel a road at night, but Sir Jaket nodded.

"And," I continued, "if we take the lad from his home in

the dark of night, the man who seeks him harm will not know he is away, nor where he has gone."

"I will leave word with the porter," the abbot said, "that he should expect your return about the time for vigils."

"That would give us enough time to wait until dark before leaving Bampton," I said. "The felon who seeks to harm William will probably obey curfew, not wishing to draw attention to himself – although I cannot be sure of that, as he did try to burn the house of the lad's parents last night."

"A desperate man, then, to attempt to burn a house in the night. When the lad's family were within asleep, I presume."

"Aye, just so. And this worries me. What next will the desperate man do?"

"The rogue abducted Sir Hugh's daughter some days past," Sir Jaket said.

"What? Is the lass safe?"

"Aye," I replied, "she managed to free herself. But since then my Kate has been bowled over in the street of a night and then I, thinking a fox had got into Kate's hen coop, was mayhap drawn into a dark toft for nefarious purposes."

"The abbey is at your disposal. This is indeed a matter of life and death. Brother Gervase, our novice master, will be told to make ready a place for the lad. As for you, the guest master will have the guest chamber ready, so you will not be required to return to Bampton in the night."

This was a generous offer, but I hesitated to accept it. To do so would mean Kate being alone with Gilbert for the night.

Sir Jaket noticed my reluctant response and understood the reason. "Janyn and Adela, if told why, would surely be willing to spend the night at Galen House. Uctred also. Your Kate will be safe should any man learn that you are absent."

These words reassured me. I told Abbot Gerleys that we would accept his offer of lodging for the night, then bade him good day. There was much to do before nightfall, so we must make haste.

I dismounted where Church View Street meets Bridge Street, sent Sir Jaket and Thomas on to the castle with instructions to meet me at Galen House when 'twas dark, then walked hurriedly to my home.

Kate was not pleased to learn that I planned to return to Eynsham Abbey that night, nor was she happy to suppose that she might be left alone. I explained that she would, if they agreed, have Janyn, Adela, and Uctred with her for the night. This information mollified her. And the three did agree.

The next visit was to Philip Lacy's hovel. If he would not allow William to go with me to Eynsham Abbey, all other schemes would amount to nothing.

"Don't much like the idea," Philip said after I told him of the plan. "But if 'e ain't safe in an abbey, 'e won't be safe nowhere. What if that fellow what tried to burn me 'ouse don't know William's away an' tries again?"

"Folk of the Weald are soon likely to learn that the lad's not at home. You must make sure this is known, but tell no one where he has gone. Friends will pry, but do not answer. Your house will be safe, I think, from further attack if the man who seeks to do William harm knows he is not within."

"You don't know who the knave is what wants William dead?"

"Not yet. I have my suspicions, but I cannot send a man to the castle dungeon without more proof of his perfidy."

William stood behind his father and had heard this conversation. I watched the lad's face to see if he was troubled by what he had heard. It did not seem so. His expression remained bland.

"I will return after dark," I said. "William will ride behind me on a palfrey from the castle marshalsea. Sir Jaket and his squire will accompany us."

Chapter 13

Friday was but two nights from a full moon, so our party would have light to see the way to Eynsham. Of course, this would also mean that a man defying curfew might see us leave Bampton. This could not be helped. If I waited for a moonless night to spirit William away it might be too late.

Janyn, Adela, and their babe arrived at Galen House only a few moments before Sir Jaket, Thomas, and Uctred. Kate and Gilbert were secure, and I departed for the Weald and Philip Lacy's home with an assurance that my wife and child were as protected as could be.

The waxing gibbous moon had just cleared the stark, bare branches of the wood to the east of Bampton when I rapped upon Philip's flimsy door. It was opened immediately.

Philip peered into the night to be sure of who was at his door. He saw me, then stood aside and whispered for William. The lad appeared, and although 'twas dark in the shadows of the interior I thought I saw him tremble. Was he concerned for his safety, or excited to be traveling some distance? Likely the lad had never been farther from home than St. Andrew's Chapel in the east or Cowley's Corner to the west.

I led William back to Galen House, keeping to the shadows as much as possible. The palfreys and Sir Jaket's ambler remained with Sir Jaket and Thomas at

Galen House. I did not want a stray whinny or iron-shod hoofbeats to awaken folk in the Weald. Horses are rare there, and their presence would likely cause residents to rise from their beds and peer out through cracked doors.

'Twas a pleasant night, if cool, and I would have enjoyed the journey but for the worry of highwaymen in the night and concern that I was doing the right thing to keep William Lacy safe.

The abbey porter had been told to expect us, and was ready to open the gate. I heard the precentor thumping the tabula to call the monks to vigils as we passed under the gatehouse.

A lay brother took charge of our beasts, and the novice master, excused from vigils for the duty, took charge of William. The lad looked around him in bewilderment. He was in a place no youth of his station would ever expect to be. I sympathized. He probably felt much as I had when I was called to London to serve Prince Edward of Woodstock some years past.

I did not have opportunity to see William Lacy again before we made our departure from the abbey at dawn. The guest master had sent a novice at first light with loaves and ale, with which Sir Jaket, Thomas, and I might fortify ourselves for the return to Bampton. I was confident as we mounted our beasts that I had secured William's safety. So the journey home to Bampton was pleasant but for the cold rain which began to fall as we neared St. Andrew's Chapel.

Uctred took my palfrey and accompanied Sir Jaket and Thomas to the castle. Janyn, Adela, and the babe remained in Galen House, by the fire, waiting for the rain to stop. It would be a long wait, as this was the kind of drizzle which, once it began, seemed never to stop.

Adela was never a lass hesitant to carry her part of a conversation, and my Kate is also a voluble woman. Janyn and I listened as Kate and her former servant reviewed town gossip. A man can often learn things by listening to his wife.

Beatrice Motherby, Adela said, had tried to convince her husband Maurice to visit me to have his sprained ankle examined. A man with a lame foot, she had complained, would find it difficult to work now that planting time was near. He'd need to use his dibble stick to keep himself upright, Beatrice had said.

"I 'eard he'd taken up with another woman," added Adela.

My ears pricked up. This was news to me.

"Who could the lass be?" my wife enquired. "Everyone knows everyone around these parts. They'd have to be like ghosts in the night to carry on so. And then surely someone would notice their nocturnal wanderings."

"One man's quite enough for me," Adela said with a chuckle. "I've no need of another, especially one with a lame foot!"

I wondered how Adela would feel if it proved true that the rumors about Maurice instead applied to her dear father. Stephen Parkin certainly appeared to have something to hide, but exactly what I knew not.

No rain lasts for ever. It only seems so. Janyn, Adela, and their babe eventually departed for the smithy, and Kate and I were left with Gilbert. Kate had prepared mussels in broth. As she was not to leave Galen House alone, I wondered how she had come by the makings of the dish.

She knew what I was thinking. "I sent Adela to the fishmonger," she explained, "and told her to keep some back for herself and Janyn."

Gilbert stuffed bits of chopped mussels into his mouth with both hands. He continues to show evidence that he will develop a hearty appetite, like John. Like his father, for that matter.

Lent was but three days off, when there would be forty days of fasting. By Easter I would be heartily tired of pea and bean pottage, and loaves with no butter. Of course, Kate may find some stockfish at the fishmonger, but the price would be dear, as others in the realm would also seek something edible to break the monotony of peas and beans and barley pottage flavored with onions and leeks.

Maurice Motherby's ankle must indeed be causing him grief. Mayhap he had broken one of the many bones which constitute a man's ankle. If so, walking on the offended appendage would not speed its healing, even if the fellow supported himself with his dibble stick.

Peas and beans would not be planted for another month. By that time a sprained ankle would surely heal, and even a broken bone would mend, or nearly so, in thirty days.

"Did like you said," Philip Lacy told me as we met departing St. Beornwald's Church after mass the next day. "Folk saw William wasn't with us when we come to church, so I told 'em 'e was away. Didn't say where. Folks be nosy an' want to know, but I wouldn't say nothin'."

Kate prepared ravioles for our dinner. She went about the work silently, the joy of her life gone with Bessie and John. I praised the meal, but this did little to cheer her. I would not have my vivacious wife back until I found the felon. And I would soon lose my livelihood if I failed at the task. I had best get at the business.

I felt sure that I knew the rogue I sought. I did not learn until later that events were being set in motion which would confirm my suspicion and provide the proof I pursued.

Three days later, the first day of Lent, I had just finished a bowl of beans yfryed, another silent meal, when I heard a robust thumping upon the door of Galen House. I opened it to find two lay brothers from Eynsham Abbey there.

"Abbot Gerleys would have you call on him," one said. "'E told us to tell you a suspicious fellow was seen at sext yesterday, an' you should know of it."

"Yesterday? Is he there yet today?"

"Don't think so. Abbot didn't say. Will you come?"

"Aye. If you set out immediately you will return to Eynsham before dark. Tell the abbot I will visit him tomorrow."

Whether or not Sir Jaket would be willing to accompany me again to Eynsham I did not know. He and Thomas would not be eager to do so if there was rain. I walked to the castle, found Lord Gilbert, reported to him that I was suspicious of one of his tenants but had not yet enough evidence to detain the man and send him to the King's Eyre, then asked his sanction for Sir Jaket and Thomas to accompany me to Eynsham, were they willing. He gave it, and they were willing.

Sir Jaket and Thomas met me at Galen House next morning with their mounts and an extra palfrey. Sir Jaket again rode his excellent ambler, a beast of which he is inordinately proud.

The sky was clear with but a few scattered clouds, so we did not have a cold rain to chill our journey. The road, however, was deep in mud, so we slowed our pace to avoid arriving at the abbey spattered with mire.

'Tis but eight miles from Bampton to Eynsham, so even though we held to a slow pace to avoid mud stains on our chauces, we arrived just as the monks had concluded terce. We waited at the gatehouse whilst a lay brother was sent to tell Abbot Gerleys we had arrived.

He was evidently expecting my arrival, for hardly had the lay brother disappeared on his errand when the abbot appeared.

"I give you good day," I greeted the abbot. "You sent for me. Something about a suspicious man lurking about the abbey, I was told."

"Indeed. Come to my chamber and I will tell you of it."

Abbot Gerleys motioned to the benches where we had sat a few days past, took his place, then spoke. "We at Eynsham Abbey have nearly two dozen corrodians. I know them well. Two days past, a new face appeared at mass. I thought perhaps the man was a new corrodian, admitted to the abbey by Brother Simon."

"The prior?" I asked.

"Aye. He has authority over such matters. I thought due to his multiple duties he had neglected to tell me of this new arrangement. At dinner on Tuesday I asked Prior Simon about the new corrodian. The man was not present for the meal, which surprised me, as most folk who enter such a bargain will not neglect an opportunity to fill their belly. Prior Simon did not know of whom I spoke.

"When we finished our dinner and left the refectory, I thought I saw a man in the cloister, ducking behind the night stairs near to the chapter house. Then I decided 'twas my imagination, but as I approached the night stairs, I heard a scream from the dormitory. A moment later I saw a man come flying down the stairs. He must have injured himself, for his steps were unsteady as he passed the chapter house.

"I did not know whether to chase after the fellow or find who had screamed. I decided to seek who had cried out, so hurried up the night stairs. There I found William Lacy clutching his throat. The lad has a cot with the novices, although whether he can be instructed in the duties of a monk is not yet decided. But you were correct. With the novices in the retrochoir, he sings, they do say, like an angel."

"Could the lad say who it was who tried to throttle him?"

"Nay. Said the man came up behind him and only fled when he howled for help. Saw the scoundrel's back as he scrambled down the night stairs.

"'Tis well that the rogue did not lay a cudgel across the lad's head," the abbot continued. "Knocked senseless, he could not have screamed. No doubt the fellow used his hands because 'twould have been noted if he'd walked the abbey with a club in his hands."

"Aye," I agreed. "Little use for such a weapon in an abbey, so 'twould be thought strange. This happened two days past?"

"Aye."

"And William has been safe since then?"

"Aye. Have you an opinion as to who the assailant might be?"

"I do. But how he discovered that William was here in the abbey, I do not know. We took the lad from Bampton in the night, with no one to see. So I thought."

"What is the man's name?" Abbot Gerleys asked.

"Maurice Motherby. I believe he has slain two lads in Bampton, and a plow team companion, or so I believe."

"Why would he do so?"

"He was seen poaching fish from the brook which flows through Bampton. 'Twas thought at first 'twas one of the lads, Kendrick Wroe by name, who was the poacher. Kendrick was a friend of the other slain lad, Thomas Rous, and of William too. There is also some suspicion that Maurice has been partaking in secret assignations with a lass in the early morn or at nightfall, though this is merely heresay. I fear that Kendrick saw the pair and told his friends before Maurice could silence him. And somehow Peter Mainwaring must have become privy to his plow mate's dealings and threatened to make them known.

"In each case, Maurice has used great guile to do murder in such a way that no one should ever suspect. There was a barely noticeable stab wound beneath Kendrick's arm that made me question the cause of death. Thomas's death was more clear cut, but Peter died by adder bite. I should never have suspected anything was amiss had I not seen the fang marks upon Peter's ankle, and later witnessed Maurice dispatching an adder in a field as if it were nothing but a wriggling worm.

"I discovered a net close to Kendrick's body that pointed to the lad poaching, but no doubt it was Maurice committing the crime rather than the youth. And later I discovered the same rope used to make the net close to the site where my kidnapped daughter Bessie had been tied to a tree. I cannot prove that Maurice did either crime, but the evidence certainly points in his direction. The only crimes I cannot yet tie him to are the attack on my wife and son, whom some villain – no doubt Maurice or someone in his employ – knocked to the ground, and the attempted burning of William's family home. I am sure each of these acts was committed by the same wicked man, but the evidence has so far eluded me. No doubt the rogue has fled abbey precincts and is even now on his way to Bampton."

"Aye, likely. If he is not already there. It is a shame you have insufficient evidence against the man to bring him before the King's Eyre."

"Aye. What *I* believe is one thing. What I may convince a judge of is quite another."

"We will keep a closer watch on the corrodians who attend mass," Abbot Gerleys said. "I can promise you that."

"How Motherby learned that William is here I cannot guess, but someone has a loose tongue."

After a simple lenten dinner of peas pottage, we bade the abbot good day, claimed our beasts at the abbey stables, and set off for Bampton. I did not expect to overtake Maurice Motherby on the road. He'd had two days' head start, and even with a limp he should have been home before we set out for Eynsham that morning.

Or so I thought. I have been wrong in the past.

As before, I sent Sir Jaket and Thomas to the castle with the beasts and walked to Galen House. Kate had barred the door, so I had to wait 'til she was sure who had rapped upon it before I could enter. A pea and bean pottage was simmering on the hearth.

"Philip Lacy has been here," she said. "Several times."

"What did he want?"

"You. I told him you were not at home."

"Did he ask to enter? Or for you to take a message?"

"Nay. Each time he said he'd return. I suspect he will do so again before dark."

Chapter 14

As usual, Kate was correct. The shadows were growing long when I heard a thumping upon the door of Galen House. I opened and saw Philip, cap in hand and tugging a forelock.

"My Margery," he began without preamble, "'as gone an' told folk where William is. Couldn't resist. Not often a cotter's lad from the Weald gets took to an abbey. She bragged on 'im, bein' proud, like. So the man what wants to slay 'im knows where 'e is, or will soon enough."

"He does already. I wondered how he had learned of it."

"Well, now you know. Is the lad safe, even though 'is place is found out?"

"Aye. He is safe."

I did not tell Philip of the danger his wife's wagging tongue had brought to her son. When the lad returned home – *if* he returned home – he could tell her himself.

Friday morning, Kate and I broke our fast with maslin loaves and ale. Kate claimed little appetite and ate but a small portion of her loaf. She was morose, as she had been since Bessie and John went to live in the castle, but seemed cheered when Gilbert, with obvious satisfaction, stuffed what remained of her loaf into his mouth.

Shortly after, about the second hour, as I was wondering how to confront Maurice Motherby, the decision was taken out of my hands. A vigorous thumping drew me to the door of Galen House, where I found an angry Beatrice Motherby.

"What 'ave you done with me 'usband?" she cried. "'E's been gone three days now."

"Gone?" I said stupidly. Well, 'twas early morning and my wits are dull at such an hour.

"Said you was seekin' to lay the blame for the evils what've come to Bampton on 'im, so 'e was goin' away for a few days. Said 'e'd return yesterday, but 'e didn't, did 'e? Said 'e was goin' to seek the man what done the wickedness you was thinkin' of layin' on 'im."

"I know where he went," I replied, "and I know whom he sought. But 'twas not a man. 'Twas a lad."

"A lad? Who?"

"William Lacy."

"Him whose mother's boastin' about 'er son bein' took into Eynsham Abbey? What would Maurice want with 'im?"

"To slay him."

"What? Why would 'e do so?"

"Because he believes William has evidence against him for three murders. And perhaps also, I am sorry to say, a dalliance with a young lass. Whether or not the lad does, I cannot say."

"What's a dalliance?"

"An assignation. A tryst."

Beatrice looked at me blankly. I decided not to enlighten her by using cruder language she might more readily understand. If she knew not of an illicit affair, I would not be the one to tell her.

This conversation had taken place whilst Beatrice and I stood at the open door. A cold draft chilled the house. I invited her into the hall, closed the door, and bade her sit on a bench. She had become much subdued.

"You live with the man. Had you no suspicions regarding his felonies?"

Beatrice remained silent. I saw a tear trickle down first one cheek, then the other. The woman's brave mask crumbled before my eyes.

"A wife," she finally said, "wants to believe good of 'er 'usband."

"But in your heart you knew, did you not, of his misdeeds?"

Another extended silence.

"Did you not wonder where Maurice came by the fish he had poached from Shill Brook? Or why he kept disappearing at first light and under the cover of darkness?"

More silence.

"Feared to ask," she eventually said. "We'd 'ad fish for fast days, an' that were enough. And whenever 'e went out 'e told me 'e was on some errand or another. I 'eard the rumors, but I'd rather not know what 'e's up to often times."

"And when Kendrick Wroe was found dead and folk thought he was the poacher, did you not then have questions for Maurice? Or when a young woman was sighted wandering down by the brook alone while he was also abroad?"

"Kept it all to meself. 'E'd always 'ad an eye for the ladies, but I never thought 'e'd act on it."

"And when my Bessie was taken, did you not suspect that Maurice might know something of her abduction?"

"'E done that too?"

"So I believe. He thought even then that I suspected

him, and desired that my attention be diverted from him to the recovery of my daughter."

Another period of silence followed.

"You last saw Maurice on Tuesday?" I said.

"Aye. Was to be 'ome yesterday, like I said. Fear somethin' bad's 'appened to 'im."

"Mayhap he has decided to flee rather than return and do the sheriff's dance. In three days he could lose himself in London."

"Would take 'im longer than that. Hurt 'is ankle, 'e did. 'E's walkin' with a limp now. But if 'e's up and gone, who'd provide for me an' the children?"

I knew that Maurice and Beatrice had two lads and a lass. "It may be that Maurice is more concerned about his neck than your stomachs. I'll not seek him in London," I said, "but perhaps he has hidden himself away between here and Eynsham. I'll collect a few grooms from the castle and seek for some trace of him. Tomorrow."

"Tomorrow? But the roads ain't safe. 'E could be lyin' injured somewhere, what with 'is bad ankle."

"I suppose he could. But if the roads are unsafe, 'tis because scoundrels like Maurice have made them so."

I felt sure that the murders of Kendrick Wroe, Thomas Rous, and Peter Mainwaring were now solved. And I knew why Kendrick and Thomas had been slain, so I thought. They had most likely learned of Maurice's poaching of Lord Gilbert's fish and demanded a portion of the takings to keep silent. And perhaps they had also threatened to tell of his flirtation with the unknown lass. Whether the latter was true or not, that was the only reason I could think of for the murder of Peter Mainwaring, which I was sure he had committed with the help of a captured adder. Only something that threatened to tear his family and livelihood apart could have caused such a falling out between previously amicable partners.

Near to dark I sought Maurice Motherby's house to learn if perchance he had returned. He had not. I left Beatrice with the understanding that if Maurice did not return in the night she would appear at Galen House in the morning with the news. I felt sure I would hear a knock on the door before full daylight brightened the town, and so I did.

Beatrice stood at the door when I opened it. "'E ain't 'ome," she said.

"I'll take men from the castle to search the road between here and Eynsham. But that is all. I'll not travel beyond Eynsham, and certainly not to London to seek him. Nor even to Oxford, although I doubt he'd go there. Too close to home and too great a chance that someone would recognize him."

Kate heard this conversation, and once Beatrice had departed she spoke. "If Maurice went to London, might he not someday return to seek revenge? You have upset his life. Might he want vengeance for this? While he yet lives, we can never be sure that he will not show himself again at Galen House."

"If he did return," I said, "I'm sure 'twould not be to show himself. Rather, he would come in the night."

"That," Kate said, "is no comfort to me."

"Nor me," I agreed. "Continue to bar the door. I'm off to the castle to gather men for the search."

"You really believe the man might've been attacked on the road between here and Eynsham?"

"Nay, but so long as it is possible, I should seek him. Or his corpse, if highwaymen found him alone."

"Would he travel to Eynsham with enough coin to make robbing him worthwhile?"

"Thieves would not know until after they had laid a cudgel across his pate or slid a blade between his ribs."

"Oh, aye," Kate agreed.

I broke my fast with a maslin loaf and ale, then hurried to the castle to gather a search party. I stepped under the portcullis and saw Sir Jaket crossing the castle yard. He greeted me and asked what I was about. I explained.

"Thomas and I will accompany you," he said, "and see this matter to its conclusion."

"If the rogue has not fled to London," I replied, "which his wife believes he would not do, for his aching ankle."

"I wonder how he came by that," Sir Jaket said.

I had no doubt now that Maurice Motherby was the man I had pursued down Church View Street but a few nights ago, under cover of darkness. The fellow had stumbled into a channel cut across the street but had regained his feet before I tumbled into the mud myself and lost his trail.

Sir Jaket on his ambler and Thomas and I on palfreys set out toward Eynsham. We did not trouble ourselves to call out for Maurice, for if he was between Bampton and Eynsham and alive, he would not want to be found.

We had just passed Yelford, walking the horses slowly and searching the verge for signs that a man might have been waylaid, when I saw the crows. I had been so intent upon examining the fringe of the road that we were nearly upon the birds before the flapping of wings as they left their perch caught my eye. Carrion crows had led me to a corpse some years past. They did so again.

I dismounted under the tree in which the crows had perched, walked a few paces into the undergrowth, and there found Maurice Motherby. Crows had plucked out his eyes and begun to devour his face. 'Twas a most repulsive sight.

"Haven't heard of thieves being active along the roads around Bampton," Sir Jaket said as he gazed upon the corpse.

"Nor have I," I agreed. "Nevertheless, 'tis likely that such rogues are active, mayhap passing from one town to another, seeking prey as they do."

Another thought came to me, which I kept to myself. I could name at least two individuals who would be pleased to hear that Maurice Motherby was on his way to the churchyard. Aymer Rous might have sought vengeance if he'd heard that Maurice Motherby had to do with his son's death; and Philip Lacy, who knew whom I suspected of wishing to slay his son and knew where Maurice had likely gone . . . and when. Perhaps the husband or suitor of the unknown lass might also have wished to see the man dispatched. I resolved to follow these thoughts no further.

There was one more matter I wanted to explore. I pulled the shoes from Motherby's corpse and found that one foot was missing the smallest toe. Here was the man who had thrust Kate and Gilbert to the ground.

We threw Motherby's corpse over Thomas's palfrey, which did not please the horse, and delivered the body to Beatrice.

As in the past, I sent Sir Jaket and Thomas on to the castle, and made my way back to Galen House, announced my presence, and heard Kate lift the bar.

"Maurice Motherby is found," I announced. "Dead along the road near to Yelford."

"Does that mean Bessie and John may return home, and I will not have to live day to day behind barred doors?"

"Aye, and I will not need to carry my dagger wherever I go."

"There is no chance that Motherby was innocent of the evils which have befallen us and others?"

"None. I was not completely convinced of his guilt until I learned that he had assaulted William Lacy at Eynsham Abbey. Abbot Gerleys said that the man who did so limped. Motherby limped, and had done so for many days. And the corpse is missing the small toe on the right foot, as you discovered when I grasped the shoe of the man who shoved you and Gilbert to the mud."

"I wonder," Kate mused, "why he decided to return to Bampton from the abbey."

"'Tis a mystery," I agreed. "Mayhap he was over-confident that I could not identify him as the source of the abominations which have brought such woe to Bampton. Or perhaps some young lass awaited his embrace. It may be that he simply could not entertain the thought of walking to London, there to lose himself. Where else," I said, "was he to go but home, and there hope to bluster through any accusations which might come his way?"

The Lord Christ bestows various talents and abilities on different men. William Lacy was not endowed with bulging muscles and great strength, as was Janyn Wagge. For recompence, the puny lad was granted a marvelous voice and a quick wit.

Abbot Gerleys told me a few weeks later, when I called at the abbey to learn when William might return home, that the lad wished to remain. "Some weeks past," the abbot said, "he could neither read nor write. Now he can do both passably well, and begs the sacrist to teach him

Latin. And he has memorized the chants for the canonical hours."

"You think he might yet make a copyist?"

"Indeed."

"His parents have no coin to buy him a place at the abbey."

"This I know. But this house is not poor, and we can accept a novice who has gifts which will supplant the funds he does not have."

So William Lacy remained at Eynsham Abbey, and there pursued a vocation. So far as I know, there was no more poaching of fish from Shill Brook. And Bessie and John returned home, their heads filled with tales of life in a castle. Bessie in particular seemed to enjoy relating the achievements of Charles de Burgh.

"He calls her 'Lady Elizabeth'," John said, and rolled his eyes.

The following autumn, shortly after Martinmas, Richard Sabyn accused Geoffrey Fraunces of stealing a ham from his smokehouse. The resulting quarrel complicated my life and brought discord to Bampton as folk chose sides in the dispute. 'Twould have simplified my life had I simply spent a shilling of my own coin to purchase a ham for Richard and placate him for his loss. Town arguments became heated, noses were bloodied, skulls cracked, teeth loosened, and friendships fractured.

And then a man died. In most unusual circumstances.

Afterword

Many readers of the chronicles of Hugh de Singleton have asked about medieval remains in the Bampton area. St. Mary's Church is little changed from the fourteenth century. The May bank holiday is a good time to visit Bampton. The village is a Morris dancing center, and on that day hosts a day-long Morris dancing festival.

Village scenes in the popular television series *Downton Abbey* were filmed on Church View Street in Bampton. The town library became the Downton hospital, and St. Mary's Church appeared in several episodes.

Bampton Castle was, in the fourteenth century, one of the largest castles in England in terms of the area enclosed within the curtain wall. Little remains of the castle, but for the gatehouse and a small part of the curtain wall, which form a part of Ham Court, a farmhouse in private hands. The current owners are doing extensive restoration work, including excavating part of the moat.

Gilbert, Third Baron Talbot, was indeed lord of the manor of Bampton in the late fourteenth century.

Mel Starr